THE MATH INSPECTORS

MYSTERY, ADVENTURE, HUMOR... and MATH!

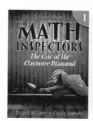   

Praise for the Math Inspectors:

"Clever, humorous, and well-written detective mystery series for elementary and middle school readers. The plot kept me guessing and entertained." - B.M.

"This is a fun math series for the eight to tween set with well developed characters who could jump onto the Saturday morning TV screen and find a comfortable home on PBS." - C.Q.

"I bought this for my 10 year-old son who is a voracious reader and loves mysteries, and he just loves the series. It makes math a fun challenge, not a chore, and still managed to entertain my bright child!" -R.B.

TO LEARN MORE VISIT

www.TheMathInspectors.com

THE MATH INSPECTORS

BOOK FIVE

The Case of the
Forgotten Mine

Daniel Kenney & Emily Boever

TRENDWOODPRESS

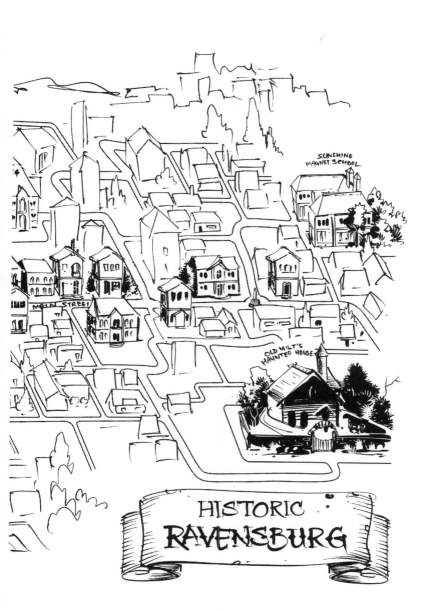

SUNSHINE
MAGNET SCHOOL

MAIN STREET

OLD MILT'S
HAUNTED HOUSE

HISTORIC
RAVENSBURG

Editing by David Gatewood, www.lonetrout.com
Interior Layout by Polgarus Studios, www.polgarusstudio.com
Cover Design by www.AuthorSupport.com
Illustrations by Sumit Roy, www.scorpydesign.com

Dedication:

To my brothers.
Daniel Kenney

To Jaime, my very first partner in crime. What adventures we have had!
Emily Boever.

Table of Contents

CHAPTER ONE

JULY 15, 1832

The moon was big and bright and bold. Not a cloud in the sky. He'd needed the lamp inside the mine, but out here, he didn't need it at all. He could see the black powder trail clearly. From his feet, it wound a hundred feet across the dirt and rocks to the mouth of the cave.

The cave that led to the mine.

When he'd been told what had to be done, he'd protested.

At first.

Then he saw the wisdom of this rather radical solution.

His partner was a no-good scoundrel. But he was also smart. And this time, he was probably right. There were starting to be rumors. And the worst thing that could possibly happen was for people to learn the truth. Better to cover up their secret.

And then, when no one was paying attention to

Forgotten, it would be easy to sneak back in, open up the mine, and retrieve what was rightfully theirs.

He crouched down, struck a match, and lit the candle. He held the small blaze over the black powder.

He hesitated.

He took one last look at his precious mine.

Then he held the candle to the powder.

The powder ignited immediately, and the flame flew across the ground toward the mouth of the cave.

He stepped back and braced himself for what would come next. But what he heard caused his heart to sink. He leaned forward and tilted his ear to the mine.

He heard it again.

Without thinking, he chased after the black powder flame, trying to catch it, to put it out. But he was no match for its speed. The flame raced furiously into the mouth of the cave.

He'd made it no more than ten feet when the cave exploded.

CHAPTER TWO

THE COMMODORE GOLDEN WING

The train wound its way through the thick trees and rocky hills of West Virginia. Looking out the windows on one side, Stanley could see the dark blues of the river that formed the canyon they were in. Looking out the windows on the other side, he could see the sun peeking through the trees as it began its descent toward the horizon. The view was so beautiful that Stanley paid no attention to the conversation around him until Felix leapt out of the seat next to him.

"Wish me luck," he said as he took off down the packed rail car. "I'm off to fulfill my destiny!"

Gertie raced after him on her short legs. "But why do you think the train conductor's going to give you golden wings?" she said, sounding exasperated. She grabbed his arm and turned him around.

"Because," Felix said, "that's just the kind of thing firemen, pilots, and train conductors do for cute, adorable kids like myself."

"But wings? Why would a *train* conductor give you *wings*? Wouldn't it make more sense to give you... I don't know, a golden wheel or something like that?"

Felix threw up his hands. "For the last time. This train is called the *Commodore Golden Wing*. Named after railroad magnate Cornelius 'The Commodore' Vanderbilt. When it was built, the *Golden Wing* was the fastest passenger train of its kind."

Now it was Gertie's turn to throw up her hands. "But trains don't even *have* wings!"

"Well, when I'm proudly wearing my golden train wings, we'll see who's laughing then." He held the door open for Stanley and Gertie, and the three of them walked into the next car.

"Don't get your hopes up too much," Stanley said. "We probably can't even get anywhere near the engine." He stopped and looked back at Herman, who had just come up behind them. "We can't, right?"

"Near the engine?" Herman said. "With this conductor? I don't think so."

"Where have you been, anyway?" Felix said.

"I was doing stuff," Herman said.

Stanley and Herman exchanged a curious look.

Gertie crossed her short arms. "Stanley, what was that all about?"

"What was what about?"

"That little look you and Herman just gave each other. You had Herman case the train, didn't you?"

Stanley turned slightly red. "For the record, the most famous mystery novel of all time, written by mystery queen Agatha Christie, took place on a train. Bad things *do* happen on trains sometimes. So I want to be prepared—to understand the lay of the land, exit points, possible suspects. You never know when we'll need to spring into action and solve a—"

"Yes," Gertie snapped. "For the entire next week, I *do* know *exactly* when we'll need to solve a case. Never! Remember? We're on vacation!"

"I know you said that..."

"No, Stanley, *we* said that. We voted."

"But it's not like criminals take vacations. Plus, Herman really wanted to do it."

"And in case anybody was wondering," Herman said, "the train conductor has a big head of fluffy white hair under his hat. I'm talking clown hair, but white."

"Herman," said Gertie, "why would anybody wonder that?"

"Um, well, he was pretty rude to me about being near the engine car. And that got me thinking... that big fluffy head of white hair would look really cool spray-painted blue, that's all."

Stanley, Gertie, and Felix all looked at Herman in silence.

"Did I say something wrong?" Herman asked.

"Remember what we said about spray-painting things not being cool?" said Stanley.

"Does that include mean white-haired train conductors?"

"Yes, Herman. It includes mean white-haired train conductors."

"This news is tragic," Felix said. "If the conductor won't let us near the engine, how am I going to get my golden wing pin? And pull the string and go 'choo choo'? How am I supposed to fulfill my destiny?"

"Sorry to be the one to tell you," said Herman.

"We may as well keep walking up toward the engine away," Stanley said. "It's not like we have anything else to do."

"I suppose that little jab was meant for me," Gertie said. "I for one am happy to have 'nothing else to do' if it means we get a week off from fighting crime—*like we agreed*. It's been one case after another all summer long, and I'm getting burned out."

"I really wanted those golden wings," Felix said.

"Don't worry, Felix," said Herman. "There's still something good up ahead. Just trust me."

Herman led the way through the next car, which was as packed with kids as their own car. Some were playing cards, others were talking and laughing, and a few were taking in the rugged mountain scenery. At the end, a dozen kids were gathered around a boy from History Club who was telling a story.

"And it's said," the boy was saying,"that till this very day, if you walk by the mine by the light of the full moon—"

Gertie grabbed Stanley by the arm and pulled him to the next train car, yelling, "Oh, look what a neat thing there is to see in the next car!"

"What's so neat about this?" asked Stanley, looking around. "It looks just like the all the other cars."

Gertie looked nervous and pointed out the window. "But the view is so much better in here. There's not much muck on these windows."

"Muck?"

Gertie smiled. "Yep. Come on, Stanley, let's keep going."

At the end of that car, there was another member of the History Club, and he had another dozen kids gathered around him. As they were passing, they heard him say, "And it's said that, till this very day—"

Again Gertie grabbed Stanley and hurried him on to the next car.

"What's going on?" Stanley asked. "You're acting weird."

"What can I say? I just love a brisk walk through a passenger train."

But up ahead was yet another group of kids gathered around yet another History Club kid.

Gertie screamed. "For crying out loud! Would everybody just shut their yappers while we pass, please? It's far too loud for—er, enjoying this wonderful view."

Everybody in the car went silent as the Math Inspectors walked through.

The fourth car they entered was different.

"Do my nostrils deceive me?" Felix said. "Stupid question—my nostrils *never* deceive me. Actually, there *was* that one time, I was four years old, and I woke up distinctly thinking my mom was making pancakes. And then bam, I walk out to the kitchen and she's actually making waffles. My nostrils did *not* see that coming."

Herman shook his head. "And you guys think *I'm* the weird one? No, Felix, your nostrils are not deceiving you."

"Then that means we've just entered the food car!"

"I told you there was something good ahead," said Herman.

Felix stared up at the menu board with a dreamy look on his face.

The train made a sudden jerking movement, and they all fell forward a pace. Stanley bumped into a girl, who had to catch hold of an arm rail to keep from falling.

"Sorry, Gina," Stanley said, helping her stand up straight.

"That's all right," said Gina Von Grubin, leader of the History Club. "Hey, I was just going to grab some fish and chips and come find you Math Inspectors."

"Oh no you don't," Gertie snapped. "If you're looking for an audience for one of your crazy, made-up stories about things that never actually happened, you'll need to find it somewhere else."

"It's nothing like that," Gina said. She held up a bare wrist. "I think somebody stole my watch."

Stanley's eyes lit up. "What did it look like?" he asked. "Where were you sitting today? Are you positive you didn't leave it at home? How valuable was this watch? Do you know anybody who'd like to hurt you? Are you having trouble in your marriage?"

Gina was clearly confused. "Marriage?"

"Sorry," said Stanley. "I was just thinking of the kinds of questions Hercule Poirot might ask. He's a famous detective in Agatha Christie's novels."

"Would he take cases like missing watches?"

Gertie put a hand on Gina's shoulder. "No, he wouldn't. As you can see, our Stanley here is getting a little confused, and unfortunately, we can't help you. We are," she looked at Stanley, "*on vacation* right now."

"On vacation right now," an annoyingly familiar voice mimicked.

Gertie wheeled around. At a high table near the window, four well-dressed kids sipped out of teacups. One girl was particularly well dressed. Some called her beautiful.

"Partridge," Gertie growled.

Polly Partridge laughed, and the last sunlight of the day highlighted her annoyingly perfect hair. "Hello, Fertie."

"It's Gertie."

"I've heard it both ways."

Gertie growled again. Stanley noticed her fingers tightening into fists.

Polly slid off her seat and stepped toward them. "I am glad to hear you Math Nerdigans are on vacation from your little crime-solving shenanigans. Maybe there *will* be something redeeming from this weekend, after all."

"Just ignore her, Gertie," Stanley said. He turned back to Gina. "Gina, when did you last see your watch?"

"Oh, did you lose your widdle bitty watch?" Polly said to Gina. "Grow up. Somebody took a bracelet right out of my purse earlier, but do you hear me crying to the Math Defectors for help? No. From the looks of that weird-looking cook up there, it was probably her. Case closed! That was easy." Polly turned to the rest of the English Club. "Maybe we should start our own detective agency."

The kids at the high table laughed.

"You couldn't catch a cold in winter," Gertie said.

Polly growled. "Oh, that is *it*. I am tired of Smurfette Gertie here."

"Who you calling a smurf, you sentence-diagramming degenerate?"

Stanley and Herman both jumped in between the two girls before either one could throw a punch.

"Listen," said Stanley. "You both make some good points. I'm sure Polly and her team do lots of...

um... interesting... English things. And as crime solvers, the Math Inspectors have had our share of successes."

"More like dumb luck, if you ask me," said Polly.

"I'd like to see you do better," Gertie snapped. She tried to get past Herman, who was now actively holding her back.

"You are *on*, half pint," Polly said, pointing a finger at Gertie's face. "This stupid place we are going to for the week is supposed to be *full* of mysteries. We can make it simple: the first group to solve a real mystery this week gets to choose a public humiliation for the other. English versus math!"

"You're going down!" Gertie screamed.

"Having a friendly little chat, are we?" said a deep voice just over Stanley's shoulder.

Coach Carter, the new gym teacher at Ravensburg Middle School, had just stepped into the rail car, and his athletic frame took up most of the entrance.

Gertie flashed a gigantic fake smile. "Just two old friends catching up on old times."

"That's what I thought," Coach Carter said. "In that case, I'll just stand here while you two old friends shake hands and part ways amicably."

"Shake hands?" said Gertie.

Coach Carter nodded.

"Amicably?" said Polly.

"Indeed," said Coach Carter.

Gertie and Polly looked at each other. Their faces both twisted in misery.

"Hands have to touch before they can shake," said Coach Carter.

Gertie tentatively put out her hand. And though it clearly pained her, Polly did likewise.

When the hands touched, they grabbed on and began to squeeze.

"Nice grip you have there, Smurfette," said Polly, clearly struggling.

"Not—a—bad—grip—yourself, Wicked Witch of the English Club," Gertie said, straining.

"You see?" said Coach Carter. "Isn't that better?"

Polly stepped back and smirked. "To be the bigger person or not to be—that is the question. Whether 'tis nobler in the mind to suffer the slings and arrows of outrageous fortune..."

Coach Carter picked up where she left off. "Or to take arms against a sea of troubles, and by opposing end them?"

Polly looked at him incredulously. "How...? You are a... a *coach*. How do you know Shakespeare?"

"It's a dangerous thing to judge a person too soon, Miss Partridge. Now, I trust the two of you will behave yourselves on this trip." Coach Carter obviously thought this was the end of it, because he headed on through the eating car and into the car beyond.

Polly recovered quickly. The smile crept back onto her face, and she said to Gertie, "I am looking forward to settling this in Forgotten." Then she wheeled on Stanley. "But I am surprised at you, widdle Stanley, for agreeing to anything that might put you face to face with ghosts. I seem to remember an encounter with ghosts last year that did not go so well for you." She snickered and walked back to the rest of the English Club members, who were laughing loudly.

Stanley looked at his friends, confused. He suddenly had a very bad feeling. "Guys," he said, his voice starting to shake. "What did Polly mean about coming face to face with ghosts?"

Gertie took a big breath. "I'm going to need you to be brave for me, okay, Stanley?"

"Brave?" Stanley squeaked. "Gertie, what's going on?"

"Going on?"

"Yes, Gertie. Something's going on, and I need you to tell me the truth."

"The truth?" Her voice was suddenly squeaking like Stanley's. "Well, you see, the truth is—"

"I got fried chicken for everyone!" Felix yelled. He stepped up behind them all with a big tray of crispy fried chicken in both hands. "And you'll never guess what they're called, Gertie. Golden Wings!"

CHAPTER THREE

THE PLAN

Felix held a piece of crispy fried chicken in the air. "You're stunned, aren't you? I mean, I know *I* was. The woman running the food car is named Slimy Sam. At first, I thought she was a dead ringer for Frank Under. She even scooped some excess grease off her hair and threw it in the deep fat fryer. But when I got to the front of the line, she was nicer than Peach Cobbler on a Duck's Back. That's actually one of her desserts. Sounds gross, doesn't it? But I'm still tempted to try it."

He held the piece of chicken up to his chest. "If the conductor really is as mean as Herman says, I suppose I could pin *this* to my chest. And as a bonus, then I'd smell good for a change."

Felix finally stopped talking and looked at his friends. Stanley was staring at Gertie, who was staring back at Stanley.

"Did I... interrupt something?" Felix said.

"Gertie was just about to explain why Polly was

talking about ghosts," said Stanley.

Felix laughed. "So, you finally know about Fred!"

Gertie glared at him and made a slashing motion across her throat.

Herman quickly went into action. "So, Stanley," he said, "would you like to see where they keep all the extra coal? It's really, um, black!"

"No, Herman, I wouldn't. What is this about ghosts? Who is Fred? And why is Gertie punching Felix in the head?"

"FELIX!" Gertie shouted. "I thought we'd agreed to keep it a secret."

Felix shrugged. "It's all anybody's been blabbing about on the train, so I thought the cat was out of the bag."

"I *knew* it," said Stanley. "I knew you were all acting weird. You were rushing me through the rail cars so I couldn't hear what people were talking about." He'd had just about enough of this. "Who—is—Fred?" he asked slowly.

"Okay, Stanley. We'll tell you," said a voice behind him.

Stanley wheeled around. It was Charlotte. Her arms were folded, and her expression was serious.

"Guys," she said, "we've always known this day would come. I say we follow the plan. But not here."

Led by Charlotte, the Math Inspectors walked back through the cars until they found an empty booth in the corner of the last car. Charlotte and Gertie sat on one side, Herman and Felix on the other. Stanley remained standing.

"Why'd we have to come back here to talk about it?" Stanley asked.

"Because of this," said Charlotte. She reached into her backpack and pulled out a gray envelope. Across the front, in black marker, was written "The Plan." She opened up it and pulled out a piece of yellow paper.

"I still don't think this is a good idea," Gertie said.

"Maybe not," said Charlotte, "but remember: Stanley's not a little kid anymore. He's in the seventh grade. I think he can handle it."

Stanley cleared his throat. "You do realize I'm right in front of you."

"Stanley, you need to sit down," Gertie said.

Stanley didn't like the way that sounded. The only time anybody told him to sit down was when his mom informed him of his upcoming dental appointments.

"I'd prefer to stand," he said.

"But it actually says, in the plan, that we're supposed to tell you to sit down."

Stanley stood with his arms folded.

"Suit yourself," Gertie said. She took a deep breath, as if whatever followed was going to be painful. "Stanley, you wanted to know about Fred."

"Yes."

"The thing is," Charlotte said, "his full name is... No Head Fred."

There was a brief silence. Stanley sat down. "I'm sorry?" he said. "It sounded like you said No Head Fred."

"That's because I did."

"Okay... Who is No Head Fred? And why is everybody on the train talking about him?"

Charlotte put a hand on Stanley's knee. "Stanley, No Head Fred is... a ghost."

A shiver went down Stanley's spine. "A ghost? But Halloween's not for another six weeks. Why is everyone talking about ghosts?"

"Because No Head Fred isn't just any ghost," Gertie said. "He's a particularly terrifying ghost. And he lives in West Virginia. Forgotten, West Virginia."

"Y-you mean he lives in the place w-where we're going?"

"We didn't want you to find out this way," Charlotte said.

"Better just give it to him straight," Felix said

through a mouthful of chicken. "But if it upsets him too much to eat, I get his Golden Wings."

"Well, like we said, there's this ghost," said Charlotte. "His name is Fred."

"And he's got no head," said Gertie.

"Thus, No Head Fred," added Herman.

"Okay, that's actually not true," Felix said. "Fred's got a head. It's just not on his neck. I heard he carries it around."

Gertie shook her head. "Nah. My grandpa says Fred keeps his head locked up in a trunk under his bed. Only takes it out for special occasions."

"That's horrible," said Stanley.

Gertie shrugged. "I guess. But remember, Stanley, he's just a ghost. All cloudy and everything. It's not so bad."

"Yes, it *is* bad," Stanley said, his teeth chattering. "It's really, *really* bad."

"No, it's really, really cool," Felix said. He took another bite of chicken. "You know, nobody seems to know how Fred became no-headed, but *I* figure maybe somebody was messing around with a Kid-A-Pult, launched a watermelon a mile through the air, and just knocked his head clean off."

"That's the dumbest thing I've ever heard," Herman said.

"You got a better theory?" asked Felix.

"Of course. I bet Fred was ice fishing."

"Ice fishing?"

"Hear me out. He was ice fishing. And he fell into a hole in the ice. He got frozen solid."

"What's that have to do with his head?" Gertie asked.

"Just listen. So they take Fred, solid block of ice that he is, and they take him to town to thaw him out. And just as they're getting the block of ice out of the truck, they drop him on the cement—and bam, he breaks in half."

"Guys!" Charlotte shouted. "That's enough.

You're scaring poor Stanley to death."

Stanley was shaking. "Y-y-you guys are just joking... right? This No Head Fred's thing's not real, is it?"

"Stanley," said Charlotte. "The rumors about him are real. Everybody's got a story about how No Head Fred goes around scaring kids who come to visit Forgotten, West Virginia. But don't worry, Fred himself *can't* be real. And you know why?"

"Because there's no such thing as ghosts?"

Charlotte winked. "Exactly. So—you think you can handle this?"

Stanley took a deep breath. "I think so. Maybe. Actually, I *am* kind of hungry." He grabbed a chicken wing off of the tray. "But I have to ask: how long were you planning to keep this from me? The whole week?"

"That wasn't the plan," said Charlotte.

"So what exactly *was* the plan?" asked Stanley.

Gertie glanced at the paper. "First we had to keep you from hearing any No Head Fred stories before we got to Forgotten. Then we were going to smuggle in a cell phone so you could call home if you got too scared."

"The first didn't work out so well, but the second we accomplished," Felix said, pulling a flip phone from his pocket.

"What?" Stanley said. "We're not supposed to have phones this week! It's part of the whole pioneer experience. How did you get it past Coach Carter?"

Felix opened the phone and hit one of the large, colorful buttons. A children's nursery rhyme started playing. "It's not a real phone. It's one of those kiddie phones they give to toddlers. I also have a big plastic ring of keys if you think that will help. We tried to get a real phone in, but that Coach Carter is surprisingly good at frisking."

"Guys," Stanley said, "you're right. I am in the seventh grade and we've been through a lot this last year. I think I can handle a few spooky stories about this town."

Charlotte, Gertie, Felix and Herman all exchanged a look, then Charlotte shrugged and Felix wiped his mouth on his shirt and his hands on his pants. "As the Math Inspectors' expert on the Forgotten legends, I believe that's my cue," he said. "There are several spooky stories about this old town we're going to. One of them is the secret legend of the red canary."

"The red canary? What's that about?"

"A red canary."

"No, what happens in the story?"

Felix shrugged. "That's what's secret about it. I have no idea what it's about. Nobody does. Believe it or not, the only thing people know about the legend of the red canary is its name. Spooky, huh?"

"Not really," Stanley said. "A complete lack of information isn't all that scary. Unless we're talking about a math problem."

"Then you'll hate this next famous legend," Felix said. "There's an overload of information about the legend of No Head Fred, though few experts agree on any of the details. Here are the two most commonly told tales about our man Fred.

"The first one is the most boring, but just in case it's true, I'd better tell you. The story is that some guy named Fred died in a mining collapse a long time ago. And to this day his ghost tries to scare kids away so they don't die in the mines like him."

"That's it?"

Felix licked chicken grease off his fingers. "Like I said, boring. And not very likely. But this next one? I'd be willing to bet one of Mabel's Mondo shakes that this one is the real deal. Get this: a long time ago, humongous city-sized dragons ruled the world. That is, until man came along."

"And woman," Gertie added.

Felix nodded. "Man and woman were crazy about

the dragons' main food supply: glazed donut holes. But, as man and woman ate up all the glazed donut holes, the dragon population dwindled. Legend has it the last dragon in the world lived here in West Virginia, until one day a guy named Fred moved to the state. Fred ate the last deposit of glazed donut holes, thus causing the last dragon to die. But before the dragon died, it swallowed Fred, which obviously separated the poor guy from his head. Over the centuries, the dragon's intestines hardened into rock and became the mines of West Virginia. Turns out, eating the last donut hole brought a curse upon Fred, and he was doomed to wander the mines forever, looking for donut holes that aren't there. They say that anywhere you go in Forgotten, you can hear a humming noise. Apparently, it's the dragon's tummy rumbling with hunger."

"Okay, that is totally ridiculous," Stanley said.

"Who knows?" said Felix. "I also heard some stories about Fred's cousin, a guy named Three Leg Greg, that'll make your hair stand on end."

Charlotte punched Felix in the shoulder, and Gertie flicked him in the forehead with her finger.

Stanley was scared—but he was keeping it together. Felix's stories were so ridiculous, they actually helped. Stanley drifted away in thought while the other Math Inspectors changed the subject, and soon the ordinary sounds of friendship settled upon them.

Charlotte began to read a pamphlet called *Mining for Dummies*, Gertie wrote something on her notepad—probably a ghost story—and Herman practiced magic tricks with a deck of cards. Felix, of course, was happy to sit and munch on fried chicken.

Stanley, for his part, just looked out the window at the green leaves and rocky hills of West Virginia. He told himself the ghost of No Head Fred was a tall tale—as ridiculous as Felix's crazy stories.

Or at least, so he hoped.

Eventually, the view out the window included something other than forest and rock. An old wooden water tower rose up in the distance. At the same moment, the train began to slow down.

The five friends all crowded around the window. The train rounded a bend, giving them a brief view of the track ahead. Pressed up against the mountains stood a little oasis of wooden buildings and dirt roads. And Stanley thought he saw something else, too. Something—

"Look up ahead," said Charlotte. "Are those mules on the track?"

Stanley looked far up ahead. Charlotte was right. Those *were* mules on the track!

He reacted without even thinking. "Stop the train!" he screamed. He bolted away from the window, determined to race up the train to the conductor. But before he'd even taken three steps, there was a horrible sound of hissing and scraping, and the train lurched violently, throwing him to the floor.

CHAPTER FOUR

"THIEF!"

The skidding and the grinding continued for a few more seconds, then the train came to a stop.

Stanley, along with the others, rose to his feet. The whole car was in chaos. Dervin was yelling at Gina as if it was her fault he had fallen. Coach Carter was grimacing in pain, rubbing his right leg with one hand and checking his cell phone with the other.

Stanley spun around to check on his friends. "Is everybody okay?" he asked.

Felix grinned. "I'm fine. Gertie provided a soft landing."

Gertie rubbed her belly. "My stomach does not thank your knee." She glanced at her watch and shook her head in disbelief. "Seven fifteen p.m. The time I was almost killed by donkeys."

"They're not donkeys," said Herman. "They're mules."

Charlotte shook her head. "Well maybe next time they'll remember not to park their mules on the train tracks."

Nobody was seriously hurt, and soon the kids were all laughing at the experience.

Coach Carter shouted to get everyone's attention. "Time to grab your bags, kids. Looks like we have to walk the rest of the way."

The Math Inspectors grabbed their luggage and stepped off the train with the rest of the kids. The train depot was still pretty far away—maybe the length of three football fields.

"Why doesn't the train just take us the rest of the way?" Stanley asked.

"Must be the air brakes," said Felix. "After you use them in an emergency, it takes a while to reset them. I guess they figure it's just quicker for us to walk the rest of the way."

And so they walked along the rocky gravel that bordered the train tracks. Five minutes later, the town of Forgotten lay before them.

"This is so cool," said Felix.

"A genuine mining town," said Charlotte.

Gertie smiled. "Three days with nothing to do except—"

A gust of wind blew a cloud of dust into their

faces. Gertie spit it out of her mouth.

"Apparently, nothing to do but get dirty," Herman said with a grin.

Stanley looked around. They stood in a town square surrounded by wooden buildings like you might see in a western movie. Every building had a wooden porch with steps leading up to it.

Coach Carter led the kids directly across the street to a building with a sign that read "U.S. Mail." Two men and two women, all dressed in old-fashioned clothes, awaited their arrival. The two men stood and the two women sat in rocking chairs. The coach climbed the stairs and shook their hands. Then one of the men stepped forward to address the kids.

He was rotund and middle-aged, and he wore a pinstriped suit and a top hat. A gold chain hung from his breast pocket, like for an old pocket watch. He had a jovial face; somehow he seemed almost like a cartoon figure.

"My name is Mayor Goatcheese," he said, and the crowd quieted. "And yes, if you're wondering, that is my real name. Years ago, my grandpappy decided to get rid of the cheese part and just go by 'Goat.' But then all of his relatives started asking him, 'Who cut the Cheese?'"

Mayor Goatcheese laughed at his own joke, which was good, because nobody else did.

Gertie leaned in. "That might have been the worst joke in history."

Herman was smiling. "I enjoyed it."

Goatcheese continued. "Okay, tough crowd. Anyway, as mayor, I want to thank you, seventh graders of Ravensburg, for once again coming to spend some time with us. On behalf of everyone here, welcome to Forgotten. Forgotten is, as I'm sure you know, an old mining town. It's a town like the way towns used to be, and over the next few days, you'll get a chance to live like you were in the 1800s. No tablets, no phones, no internet, no TV, no movies. The only webs we have around here are made from spiders, and the only nets we have are the ones we use for fishing."

He laughed again, and Stanley saw Herman smile.

"I know, some of you are probably wondering how you'll survive. But trust me, people survived in the 1800s, and you will too. In fact, when you get back to the comforts of home, you'll wonder how you'll get along without churning your own butter!"

By looks on the faces of his classmates, Stanley figured that wasn't going to happen.

"Well, that's enough from me," Goatcheese said. "Let me introduce to you Forgotten's leading lady and its oldest citizen, the lovely Miss Nellie Juneberry."

The ancient-looking woman in the rocking chair behind him smiled and waved, but did not stand, though one gnarled hand squeezed the handle of a dark wooden walking stick. She wore a simple light blue dress and a white bonnet with a small yellow flower pinned to one side.

"Please call me Nellie," she said. "I am eighty-one years old, and believe it or not, I was born in this building behind me. I know it says U.S. Mail on the front, and that's because it's a post office. But it's also been the home of my family for over..." She laughed. "Well, I'm not sure I can count that high."

People actually *did* laugh at her joke, and Stanley could have sworn Mayor Goatcheese seemed annoyed.

Nellie continued. "Let's just say, many years ago, my great-grandmother was the postmaster of Forgotten, and that title has run in the family ever since. You're all welcome to come by for a chat with Nellie any old time you'd like. And maybe if you're lucky, I'll have an extra lollipop lying around. I do like my lollipops."

The kids clapped, and the mayor stepped forward. "I'm not sure bribery is allowed in this town, Miss Nellie. And as to what else is not allowed in this town, let's hear from our very own lawman. Please welcome Sheriff Gordon."

The man who stepped forward was maybe in his early forties. He wore a cowboy hat, boots with spurs, and had a thick handlebar mustache that stuck out past his ears. He spit something brown and gross onto the wooden porch, then stood with his legs apart and thumbs tucked into his belt buckle.

"I'm Sheriff Gordon," he said with a thick country drawl. "And you're in *my* town now." He paced back and forth, scanning the crowd with eyes narrowed, like he was looking for outlaws. "I might be dressed like a lawman from the past, but never forget one thing: I'm a *real sheriff*. That building over yonder is a *real jail*. And the copper-cased .45 caliber bullets I keep in my Colt single-action revolver? They're real too."

Felix leaned in. "Holy *Gunsmoke*, Stanley. This guy's the real deal. You can practically smell the bacon coming from his sweat. Isn't it great?"

Stanley wasn't so sure a guy trying to scare a bunch of kids by talking about his real bullets qualified as "great."

"I need you young'uns to know somethin' and know it clear. You step one toe outta line, and—well, let's just say you won't be visitin' the principal's office. Here, let me give you an example."

Sheriff Gordon peered out at the crowd. Looking for outlaws again. None of the kids moved a muscle.

Then Sheriff Gordon stopped. "You," he said, pointing over the crowd's head. "Stop right there."

The kids spun around. Behind them stood a strange-looking man in blue overalls. He was dirty from head to foot. But that wasn't what was strange about him. What was strange was the real candle on top of his hat—with the flame blazing.

He looked up at the sheriff, his eyes wide with terror.

Sheriff Gordon shook his finger at the strange man. "I don't remember seeing you round these parts, and to be honest, I don't like the looks of you. And I *definitely* don't like the looks of your hat. Hold it up, real slow like, and don't even think about doing anything foolish."

The man grabbed his hat and slowly raised it into the air. Sheriff Gordon drew his pistol lightning fast and shot before anybody even had time to realize what was happening.

The tiny light atop the man's hat flickered out.

One or two kids screamed, but most of them remained silent.

Then the man in the overalls dropped his hat to the ground, smiled, and gave the sheriff a thumbs-up. "Nice shot," he said. "Thought you might just hit my hat this time."

Stanley turned back to the sheriff and found himself clapping with the rest of his classmates.

Sheriff Gordon smiled and bowed. "Thanks, everyone. By now you've realized that my good buddy Marv there is all part of the show. The truth is, I *am* the real live sheriff of this town, but since the last crime in Forgotten was over one hundred years ago—unless you count the occasional thieving raccoon—I have to find other ways to keep my skills sharp. Like shootin' the flames off of candles." He smiled. "I'm looking forward to getting to know you kids, and I want you all to think of me as the cool sheriff you've always wanted."

The kids clapped even louder, and Sheriff Gordon stepped back, smiling.

Felix leaned in. "I'm confused. So he *is* the real deal or he's *not* the real deal?"

"Maybe what you were smelling was turkey bacon," Stanley offered.

Mayor Goatcheese came forward again. "Thanks, Sheriff. And thanks, Marv. That candle on your head makes me laugh every time. And now, students, let me introduce you to the person who will shape your week more than anyone else." He pointed at the fourth member of the group—a young lady in a long dress. "Please give a warm welcome to Miss Calloway."

Miss Calloway looked to be in her late twenties. She wore a dress that was fitted tightly around her neck, poofed a little in the back, and flowed all the way to the floor. She also wore an elegant hat. She appeared straight as a ruler, her face set in a scowl, as she strode stiffly to the center of the porch.

She spoke just as stiffly. "Most people today think they have problems. They think their lives are difficult. I'm here to tell you, boys and girls, that most people are wrong. You will find that life in the 1800s was much more difficult than you thought. Around here, mornings start very early and the work is very hard. Because of that, bedtime is also very early. In a few minutes, you will all retire to your bunkhouse for some sleep. Believe me when I say *you will need it*."

"I bet she could handle a six-shooter, too," Felix whispered.

Mayor Goatcheese stepped to the front again. "Thank you, Miss Calloway, as always, for that delightfully warm welcome. Now then, children. Miss Calloway will show you to your bunkhouses where you'll be able to settle in and get some rations."

"Rations?" said Felix, sounding alarmed. "I don't like the sound of that."

"I will just mention two rules before I let you go," the mayor said. "And I beg you to take these seriously. First, we're in the midst of the nastiest stretch of dry weather we've had in years. Everything is dry, too dry, and the whole side of the mountain is liable to go up in flames at a moment's notice. So—absolutely *no* campfires this week. The second rule is this: do not, for any reason, leave your bunkhouse at night after the bedtime bell has been rung. We are in a very remote part of West Virginia, and not only are there steep drops everywhere you look, but there are animals in these woods. *Wild* animals."

The mayor's eyes twinkled as he added, "As mayor, I can also confirm that the rumors you've heard are most *definitely* true. Something else lives among us..." He paused—and turned suddenly serious. "There are ghosts in Forgotten." Then he wished everyone the best of luck, and Miss Calloway started to lead the students to their bunkhouses.

Stanley stood rooted to the spot, terrified at the mayor's last words. He tried to tell himself the mayor was joking, like that stunt with the candle, but the way Goatcheese spoke, it didn't sound like a joke.

Charlotte laid a hand on his shoulder, and he screamed.

"I'm sorry, Stanley, I didn't mean to—"

"Poor Stanley." It was Polly, followed by her gang of English snobs, all of whom were laughing. "Without the courage to step out of his bunkhouse at night, it looks like we have this mystery competition in the bag."

"You wish," said Gertie. "First, Stanley's got more genuine courage in his little toe than you've got mathematical ability in your whole body. And second, we don't even have a mystery to solve yet."

Polly seemed unconcerned. "One will present itself. And after we win, oh, do I have a delicious humiliation picked out for you."

At that moment, the train whistled—loudly. Everyone jumped, but only Stanley screamed.

Polly laughed. "Stanley is scared of the train whistle? This is going to be even easier than I thought."

Gertie had started to respond when another scream rang out. And this one wasn't from Stanley.

It was from the post office. The old woman, Nellie, sat in her rocking chair clutching at her neck.

And she was shouting, "Thief!"

CHAPTER FIVE

THE ENGLISH DETECTIVES

Stanley, Gertie, and Polly ran to the post office porch where Nellie continued to shout. Polly's long legs carried her to the steps faster than the other two, but she still wasn't the first one on the scene. That would be Sheriff Gordon, who seemed to come from nowhere.

The sheriff laid a hand on Miss Nellie's shoulder. "Just calm down, Miss Nellie," he said. "Now's what's this about a thief?"

"My locket. My locket's been stolen!"

"Your locket? You mean you just noticed it was gone?"

Miss Nelly stood straight-backed. She thumped the wooden floor with her walking stick. "I *mean* I've worn that locket every day of my life since I was a little girl, and somebody stole it right off my neck as I was rocking in my chair!"

Sheriff Gordon shook his head in disbelief.

"While you were right here in this chair? Did you see who it was?"

"No, I did not see who it was," said Nellie. "The brute came up right behind me. To be honest, I was drifting off to sleep. I do that sometimes. And he snatched it right off my neck."

"Well, did you at least see which way he went?"

Nellie pointed an old gnarled finger down the street. "That way... I think..."

Sheriff Gordon rolled his eyes. "Okay, Nellie. I'm going after the bandit. You get yourself inside and rest." He tipped the brim of his cowboy hat and ran off.

It was only then that Nellie saw Polly, Stanley, and Gertie standing at the bottom of the steps. "Oh, I'm so sorry," she said. "I didn't mean to frighten you children. It's just, that locket... it's very dear to me."

Stanley started up the steps to launch his investigation. But then the unthinkable happened.

Polly stepped in front of him.

"I completely understand, madam," said Polly. "I am not scared; rather I am determined. Determined to solve the mystery of your missing locket. My name is Polly Partridge, and I run an organization called the English Detectives."

"*What*?" Stanley said.

Polly ignored him. "I specialize in solving crimes just like this."

"No, she doesn't!" said Gertie.

"Ma'am, my friends and I can help you," said Stanley. *"We're* the ones who solve crimes."

Polly leaned in next to Nellie. "Sorry about these kids, madam. The English Detectives have been solving crimes for years, and we have become a bit of a target. Every time I begin solving a crime, they try to swoop in and take credit for it."

"She's lying!" Gertie screamed.

But Nellie's face hardened, and she spoke to Polly, ignoring Gertie's denial. "I've known people like that," she said.

Polly held out her hand. "Miss Nellie, if you want to recover your locket, I would be willing to assist you in your investigation."

Nellie took Polly's hand. "I don't know what to say."

"I do," said Gertie. "Polly Partridge is a big fat stinking liar! She doesn't know the first thing about solving crimes."

"And you do?" said Nellie suspiciously.

"Yes," said Stanley firmly. "We do. We're the Math Inspectors. We've already solved a bunch of crimes. And I promise we can help you."

"Sounds like the desperate rantings of a lunatic if you ask me," Polly said.

Nellie stumbled, and Polly caught her arm. Nellie steadied herself against the walking stick. "I'm just so tired," she whispered.

"How would it be if I help you into your place, and you can tell me who you think might have done this to you?" Polly said.

"Oh no you don't!" said Gertie.

"Listen, Gertie," said Polly. "How about you put your anger and jealousy aside for just a moment and think about someone *else* for a change? This nice woman is grieving. And right now, she needs my help." Turning so Nellie couldn't see, Polly winked and flashed Gertie an evil little grin.

Gertie's fists were clenched, her teeth were gritted, and she looked like she was going to burst.

Stanley put a hand on her shoulder and pulled her back. "Not now," he whispered. Polly had beaten them to the punch. And Stanley could tell from the look on Nellie's face that her mind was made up. Trying to get the Math Inspectors a place at the table would not be in their best interests.

At least not tonight.

"Time for bed," said a stern voice from behind them.

Stanley turned to see Miss Calloway in all of her royal stiffness.

"I'm sorry for what happened to you, Nellie, but these kids should not be here. They need to settle in and get some sleep."

Miss Nellie grabbed Polly gently by the arm. "Thank you, dear, for your kindness. Come by tomorrow and I'll answer any questions you think might help find my locket."

"Of course." Polly smiled sweetly—sickeningly sweetly—and the kids followed Miss Calloway back to join the rest of the students.

"That was low, Polly, even for you," Stanley said.

"Whatever do you speak of, Stanley? My English Detective Agency was on the scene first. Now, if you will excuse me, my colleagues and I have an investigation to launch."

She snapped her fingers, and the English club surrounded her. They put on their sunglasses—even though it was quickly becoming dark—and blended into the crowd.

The kids followed Miss Calloway out of the square. A dirt road led to four log cabins—two small, two large.

"Boys to the left, girls to the right. Coach Carter will be in this smaller building, and I will be in that other one, should there be anything that you truly need. And I do mean *truly*. Don't bother us if you're cold, tired, thirsty, or bored. Life was tough in the old days, and I'd suggest you get used to it. Oh, and be sure to get a good night's sleep. Morning will come early, and you'll need to be well rested for your chores."

"Chores?" Gertie murmured.

"One more thing. Mining towns in the 1800s didn't have a lot of running water, and neither will you. If you need to use the restroom, head to the outhouses." She smiled for the first time that day. "They're behind the bunkhouses."

"Outhouses?" said Felix, his eyes wide.

"And you can fetch yourselves some water from the well."

"Is she kidding?" asked Stanley.

"I don't think so," Charlotte said.

Calloway looked out over the crowd. "Good night, children, sleep tight, and most importantly... *don't let the scary ghosts bite.*"

CHAPTER SIX

NO SUCH THING AS GHOSTS

The bunkhouse looked exactly like Stanley thought an old bunkhouse in a mining town would look. Simple wooden bunk beds lined the long walls, with an aisle down the middle.

As he entered, school bully Dervin Chowder was thumping on his chest and shouting.

"I am Dervin, Lord of the Bunkhouse! You all see those four bunk beds right here? These are *my* beds. Does that mean some of you will be sleeping on the floor tonight? Yes, it does. Do I care about that one bit? No, I don't."

The boys scrambled to claim beds, and when the dust settled, Felix, Herman, and Stanley were the odd men out. All the beds had been taken, and they were left standing with no place to sleep.

Felix opened a drawer on a dresser at one end of the bunkhouse. "You know, guys, I don't think I'll fit inside this. You think we could just beat Dervin up?"

The three friends looked down the aisle. Dervin was lying on his back and lifting three kids into the air. This was his normal bench press routine.

"I'm not sure the whole *bunkhouse* could beat Dervin up," said Stanley.

A knock sounded on the door, and Coach Carter entered, carrying a box of cans.

"I've got your nightly rations," he said.

Felix shot his hand into the box and snatched out a can. "Corn?" he said. "Our nightly ration is corn?"

"It was either canned corn or canned beets. Consider yourselves lucky," Coach Carter said, handing out the cans.

Stanley, Herman, and Felix took their cans of corn and huddled between two of the dressers. They opened up the cans and drank from them like they were milkshakes.

"This is super gross," Herman said.

"And that means a lot coming from a kid with a crazy uncle who traps animals for a living," Felix said. "Mabel would roll over in her grave if she could see us now."

"Felix," said Stanley. "Mabel's not dead."

"And Uncle Farley doesn't trap animals," Herman added. He smiled. "Although he doesn't mind the occasional grilled squirrel from time to time."

"Not funny," said Felix.

Coach Carter handed out the last of the corn, then whistled loudly to get everyone's attention. "I'm about to leave for the night," he said. "When I do, I'm turning out the light and locking the door. I expect you all to go to bed. If I see the light on or hear any shenanigans, I'm supposed to tell Mrs. Calloway, and she *guarantees* she has something you can all do tomorrow that you will *not* enjoy."

With that, Coach Carter turned off the lights, walked out the door, and left the seventh-grade boys of Ravensburg Middle School in complete darkness. They were going to be stuck in that bunkhouse till morning.

"I've gotta be honest," said Felix. "I don't like the 1800s."

Stanley agreed. The darkness was so deep that he couldn't see a thing. Even when he waved his hands right in front of his face, he could barely see them. He told himself to wait for his eyes to adjust before panicking, but long seconds passed, and nothing became any clearer.

A soft scraping sounded from his right. Or was it his left? Surely *this* was a good time to panic.

"Felix?" he whispered. "Herman? Where are you guys?"
Silence.

That's when he heard it—a low creaking noise

followed by a thud. Seconds later, something slithered toward him.

He had just opened his mouth to scream when a hand was slapped over it.

"Quiet," Herman whispered. "Follow me. You'll want to see this."

A bit of moonlight suddenly streamed through the window, and he saw that one of the dressers had been pulled away from the wall. Judging by the shadow on the floor, it looked like Herman had crawled behind it.

Herman stuck his head through a hole in the wall. "Look, Stanley: No Head Herman."

"It's a secret door to the outside," whispered Herman excitedly. "I found it when I was trying to get cozy behind the dresser."

Felix inched closer to the hole. "You guys want to go out and explore?"

"Now?" Stanley asked.

"Why not?" said Herman.

"Because it's against the rules, and I don't want Miss Calloway to do anything to us tomorrow, and most of all..." Stanley's voice started shaking. "Because of the ghosts."

"But where there's ghosts, there's donut holes," Felix said.

Stanley frowned, retreated to the other dresser, and cuddled up with his backpack. He heard Herman and Felix whispering and then the sounds of the secret door closing and the dresser sliding back into place. He tucked himself under his jacket and tried to sleep.

Maybe it was the hard wooden floor, but no matter which way he turned, he couldn't shake the feeling that the floor was rumbling slightly. Then clouds covered the moon, and once again the room was plunged into complete darkness.

He sighed. He, Stanley Robinson Carusoe, was in the dark, on a hard floor, in a bunkhouse, with the seventh-grade boys from his school. And there just might be a ghost roaming around.

Of course, he reminded himself, *ghosts aren't real.* They couldn't be real.

But thieves? Thieves were definitely real. Somebody had stolen Gina Von Grubin's watch, and Polly's bracelet, and Miss Nellie's locket. There was a thief in Forgotten, and no matter what Polly Partridge did to get in his way, Stanley was going to figure out who that thief was.

As his eyes grew weary, his mind slowed, and for the first time that day, everything became quiet. Completely quiet. Except for the slight humming sound. Some might have called it a rumble.

He sat up to figure out where the rumble was coming from. And as he did, he saw something run by the outside of the cabin.

It was a dark and shadowy figure.

And it had no head.

Stanley and the others were awoken the next morning by a loud, ringing bell.

Felix raised his head from the floor. "It's still dark out there. What are they playing at?" He rolled back over and snuggled up against his backpack.

"That's not just a wakeup call," said a very tired

Stanley. "It's a breakfast bell."

Felix popped back up. "Breakfast? As in food?"

Herman stood up slowly. "Yeah, probably more canned corn."

The three boys put on their blue jeans and walked past the other seventh-graders, who were getting out of their bunks.

They found Charlotte and Gertie waiting for them on the dirt path. "Aren't those beds amazing?" Gertie said. "I'm pretty sure those are real goose feathers in the mattresses."

"We don't want to talk about it," Felix said.

Stanley tilted his head and listened. The humming sound was still there. A shiver went down his spine as he pictured the figure with no head running past the bunkhouse.

"Something wrong, Stanley?" Charlotte asked.

Stanley thought about telling her what he'd seen the night before... then thought better of it. *No such thing as ghosts*, he reminded himself for about the hundredth time in the last eight hours.

No such thing as ghosts.

They walked to the town square with the other seventh-graders. Everyone was too tired to talk; only the occasional yawn disrupted the pre-dawn quiet. They found the mess hall, a large log building just on the edge of the square, by following the smells of food.

Felix's eyes widened as he sniffed the air. "Is it possible?" His head bobbed up and down excitedly as they entered the mess hall. When he saw what he was looking for, he raised both hands. "It's Slimy Sam! Can you believe it? We're saved! We're saved!"

Slimy Sam had prepared a feast for them: pancakes, bacon, biscuits, gravy, and eggs. And as the kids sat down together and started eating, Stanley had to admit it was pretty fantastic. Almost good enough to make him forget about the crummy night's sleep. Almost good enough for him to forget about the strange hum and the even stranger shadowy figure. And definitely good enough to help him focus on the mystery.

"Who do you think stole Miss Nellie's locket?" he asked.

Charlotte shrugged. "Could be anybody. We don't know anything yet."

"We know that Gina's watch is still missing," said Herman.

"And we know that Slimy Sam would give Mabel a serious run for her money if she ever opened up a breakfast place in Ravensburg," Felix said. "Did I just say that out loud? Hey, guys, I'd really appreciate it if that didn't get back to Mabel, okay?"

Gertie rolled her eyes at him, as usual. "Polly's bracelet is missing too," she said. "Of course, I'd like it to stay missing for all eternity... but it *is* a data point."

"So that's all we know," said Stanley. "Three things are missing. And Miss Nellie said she was just rocking on her chair when somebody came up behind her and ripped the locket right off of her neck."

Gertie pointed her bacon at Stanley. "Miss Nellie said it was a brute who did it."

"But she never saw this brute's face," said Stanley. "So we don't know if it was a girl or a boy."

Charlotte put down her fork. "Wait, girl or boy? You think a student stole Miss Nellie's locket?"

Stanley shrugged. "Wouldn't that be most logical? Both Polly and Gina had their jewelry items stolen on the train. Then Miss Nellie has her jewelry stolen not long after we arrive."

"Okay, Stanley," said Charlotte. "Say you're right. Say it was one of our fellow students. Why now? We've gone to school with these kids our whole lives. Herman's the newest kid in our grade, and he wouldn't even do anything like that... would you?"

Herman smiled. "If Miss Nellie's hair wasn't

painted blue in the process, then probably not."

"So why, all of a sudden, is one of these kids going on a crime spree?"

Stanley scratched his chin. "Think about all the fidgety brain energy that needs to be released when kids can't spend half their time on their phones," he suggested. "Who knows what they're capable of now that they have to focus on the world around them?"

"I don't think phone withdrawal turns people into thieves," Charlotte said. "Plus, there's something else. The numbers."

Stanley dropped his fork. "What numbers?"

Charlotte smiled. "Exactly my point. All we're doing is guessing right now. We don't have any numbers."

"You're right," said Stanley. "We need numbers."

Felix raised a finger. "And we need Slimy Sam's recipe for buttermilk biscuits. It's flake after heavenly flake of buttery goodness."

"But getting solid numbers brings us to our next problem," Stanley said.

Gertie punched a fist into her open hand. "Polly."

"Exactly. She's sunk to a new low this time, pretending to be a legitimate detective agency in order to cut us out of the investigation."

Charlotte smiled. "I say we sneak out of here and

interview Nellie before Polly can get her mitts on her."

Stanley stood. "Let's do it!"

It was at that very moment that Miss Calloway entered the mess hall. "Good morning, students," she said coldly, her tone suggesting there wasn't really anything good about this morning.

A few kids responded, but most grumbled and ignored her.

Miss Calloway gave Stanley a stern look, and he immediately sat back down. Then she walked to the bell at the center of the room and rang it. It echoed loudly through the mess hall.

"I said good morning, students!" she said. "And I *always* expect to be answered."

"Good morning, Miss Calloway," answered the seventh graders of Ravensburg Middle School in unison.

She nodded. "It's time to start your education. From this moment on, you are mining children in the 1800s. Therefore, it's not reading, writing, and arithmetic that will occupy most of your time. It's mining. And since none of you has the least idea of what it's like to work the mines, it's time to go to mining school."

Felix spit out his orange juice. "Mining school?"

"And mining school starts now!"

CHAPTER SEVEN

A FUNNY FEELING

Miss Calloway marched the seventh-graders away from the mess hall, past the bunkhouses, and up the mountain to the mouth of a cave. A cool blast of air hit Stanley right before an old miner stepped out.

Stanley recognized him at once. He was the man with the candle on his hat when they'd arrived. When Sheriff Gordon had done that amazing trick shot.

"Hello, kids. My name is Marv, I run the Junior Mining Training program here. Today, I'm going to teach you as much about mining as I can. But unfortunately, it will all be in the classroom." He pointed to a large wooden barn that abutted the mountain right next to the mouth of the cave.

"But I've got one good piece of news. You see this little train here?" Marv pointed at a little train that sat in a little roundabout of track as if it was waiting to head back into the mines. It reminded Stanley of a train he'd ridden at Omaha's Henry Doorly Zoo once. Yet this one was even smaller. "I call it The Little Rascal. It's an old steam engine. And my reward for the best student today is... tomorrow, I'll give you a chance to drive her."

Felix jumped into the air and yelled, "Whoopee!"

The entire class looked at Felix while Gertie put her head down in shame. "I can't take him anywhere."

The kids spent the rest of the morning doing mining problems, learning about mining, and getting first-hand experience at being what Marv taught them were called "breaker boys and girls," which involved a crazy rock-sorting contraption. Felix was the only one who didn't get to use it, because he was too tall to sit in the little seat.

Marv patted a crestfallen Felix on the back. "Don't worry, son. I had you pegged as a nipper anyway."

"Thanks," Felix said, choking back emotion. "That's the nicest thing any crusty old miner has ever said to me. I have no idea what it means, but it was really nice."

But apart from that, Felix was indeed the best and most enthusiastic student Marv had probably ever seen, and when it came time for Marv to pick the best student of the day, it was an easy decision.

"Okay, tall and goofy," said Marv. "Looks like you're driving a train tomorrow."

Felix was about to launch into the air with another whoopee when the bell sounded in the mess hall, and the kids ran out of the mining barn and practically stampeded each other to see what Slimy Sam had cooked up for lunch.

The menu board outside the mess hall read "Spaghetti, Meatballs, and the Best Italian Sausage You Ever Done Eat." Felix fell to his knees and started weeping with joy.

Stanley wasn't quite as excited. His mom made pretty good spaghetti, and she made it all the time. So if ever there was a Slimy Sam meal he could skip, this would be it. And he had an errand to run.

He took off for the post office, bounded up the steps to the porch, and knocked politely on the door.

A minute later, the door opened, and Miss Nellie's face poked through. "Can I help you?"

"My name is Stanley Carusoe. My parents thought you might remember them."

She studied Stanley like she was trying to remember.

"My dad says I look just like him when he was in seventh grade and he came to Forgotten."

At that, Nellie's eyes lit up. "Henry? Was it Henry?"

Stanley smiled. "Yes, ma'am."

"And... oh dear, I can even picture her face. There was a girl with him. What was her name?"

"Clara. Her name was Clara."

"That's it. Henry and Clara. Those two kids bothered me quite a little that year." Nellie shook her head and sighed. "But what a long time ago that was. And then Henry sent me postcards after that. Sweet kids."

She put her hands on her hips and fixed her gaze on Stanley. "Wait, you said your parents. You don't mean to tell me those two sweet kids got married?"

Stanley nodded. "They did."

"Well, I'll be. Sometimes life just kinda works out, doesn't it?"

Stanley shrugged. "I guess."

The woman's face fell. "And sometimes it doesn't work out." She shook her head. "What can I do for you, Stanley?"

"Actually, Miss Nellie, it's what *I* might be able to do for *you*. I think we got off on the wrong foot yesterday. On my parents' honor, I really do have a detective agency called the Math Inspectors, and I really do help the police solve crimes. I think I can help you find that locket. If I could just ask you a few questions."

"Stanley, I appreciate it. I really do. If you say you're a real detective, then I believe you. The problem is, that nice Polly girl is already investigating for me. In fact, she arrived just a couple minutes ago."

Miss Nellie swung the post office door wide, revealing Polly. She was sitting on a stool inside, eating a chocolate chip cookie.

"Dear, dear Stanley," Polly said. "As I told Miss Nellie here, 'Crime doesn't sleep. And neither do the English Detectives.' Fear not, Stanley. We will solve the crime, so you can do better things—like have fun." Polly flashed a big, huge, fake smile.

"Polly's right, Stanley," Miss Nellie said. "Go eat some of Slimy Sam's Italian sausage. You won't regret it." She began to shut the door, then stopped. "Oh, and Stanley? Be sure to tell your parents hi for me."

She let the door swing closed.

Seated in front of a heaping plate of spaghetti in the mess hall, Stanley told his friends about what had happened. He expected them to be as mad at Polly as he was, but Gertie just shrugged.

"Normally, I'd be pretty upset," she said. "But this is the best spaghetti I've ever eaten in my life."

Herman nodded. "This Slimy Sam knows how to cook."

Felix smiled, his enormous face completely covered in spaghetti sauce. "All I can say is I'm happier than a Pig in Slop, which coincidentally is Slimy Sam's surprise dessert for today."

Gertie rolled her eyes. "You certainly look like a pig in slop. And Stanley, I admit I am a *little* worried about Polly solving the mystery first."

Charlotte wiped her face with her napkin. "Who cares about Polly? She couldn't find her way out of a paper bag. Let her try."

"There's another thing I've been wondering about," Stanley said. "That rumbling noise. Am I the only one hearing that? Where is it coming from? It's pretty suspicious, if you ask me."

"You're hearing suspicious rumblings?" Charlotte

said. "Maybe a vacation from crime-solving really *would* be good for you, Stanley. You should just try to have some fun."

"Fun?"

"Yes, Stanley. Fun. The thing kids do. You know, throwing balls, playing goofy games, and laughing like idiots. *Fun.*"

"I'll get the spray paint," said Herman.

Gertie snapped her fingers. "Sit, Herman, right where I can see you."

After lunch the kids were given free time, and the seventh graders of Ravensburg Middle School retired to a large grassy area between the town and the railroad tracks. Some kids played football, others played volleyball, and the Math Inspectors played the Science Inspectors in a spirited game of kickball. Charlotte remarked to Stanley that she'd never seen so many strikeouts.

"You mean in one game?" asked Stanley.

"I mean in all the kickball games ever played in the history of the world."

Stanley laughed.

"So, are you having fun?" she said.

"I guess."

"Stanley, can I ask you a question?"

"It's never a good thing when people ask you if

they can ask you a question."

"Why is it so hard for your brain to...?"

"To what?"

Charlotte smiled. "To stop?"

It was a good question. A question Stanley had thought about himself. It was hard for him to relax the way other kids did. He liked challenges. He liked problems. He liked puzzles. But one thing he didn't like to do was talk about his feelings.

"It's just who I am," he said.

Charlotte laughed. Then she punched him in the shoulder. "Yes, Stanley. I guess it is."

It was Charlotte's turn to kick, and she launched a rocket into the outfield. Two of the Science Club members ran into each other while trying to catch it, and Charlotte jogged easily around the bases.

But Stanley found himself staring past the game to the train tracks beyond.

To his right was that wooden water tower he'd seen when they first got a glimpse of town. To his left was the small train depot where the Commodore Golden Wing had already been turned around and was waiting for their return trip home. And on the other side of the tracks, munching the tall grass, were the mules. The same mules that had been standing on the train tracks when they first came into town.

Stanley pictured that scene. The mules on the tracks. The train unexpectedly stopping. Everyone falling. He looked at the spot where the mules had been standing, at the spot where the train rested now. Then he looked over at the wooden water tower.

It all felt... wrong.

Wait a second.

He stood up.

Charlotte was right. His brain never stopped working. In particular, his brain was always looking for things that didn't quite make sense. Especially when it came to numbers.

The Science Club members had apparently lost Charlotte's home run ball in the tall grass, so the kickball game was paused. That gave Stanley his chance to speak to the Math Inspectors.

"Charlotte, Gertie, Felix, Herman, I want to tell you that I've had a lot of fun."

"And now you're ready to have *more* fun?" Gertie asked.

"Of course I am," said Stanley. "But *my* kind of fun. Math Inspectors, I have a problem, and I need your help. Follow me."

As Stanley led his friends to the railroad track, he explained his funny feeling. What his friends liked to call a "Stanley."

"I don't understand," said Herman. "Isn't a train engineer *supposed* to stop the train when he sees something on the tracks?"

Charlotte met Stanley's eyes. "Just go through it one more time," she said.

Stanley took a deep breath. "Yes, a train engineer is supposed to stop the train before it can hit something on the tracks. But that doesn't mean a train engineer is supposed to hit the *emergency* brake."

"But you started screaming for him to stop the train," Herman said.

"Well, sure. But that's me. *I* would have pulled the emergency brake, because, as you all like to remind me, I'm scared of everything and I would have panicked—and I suppose I did, a little. But remember how Herman described the engineer, Captain Ron? Old guy with white hair. I'm guessing that means he's been driving trains for a while, and there's no way an experienced train engineer like Captain Ron would have panicked."

"I think Stanley's right," said Felix. "Captain Ron would have seen the mules well in advance, slowed the train down, and eased to a stop. As small as that train is and as slow as it was going, he would have had time to do that. He wouldn't have needed to yank the brake and send all his passengers to the floor."

Gertie ran her hands through her hair. "You're suggesting he didn't need to pull the emergency brake to stop the train for the mules—so you think he had some *other* reason to pull the brake? What does this have to do with anything?"

"Yeah," agreed Charlotte. "Why does this matter?"

Stanley frowned. "Why does it matter? Why does it *matter*? It matters because... because... well, I don't know why it matters. It just doesn't add up. And I think we should go talk to Captain Ron and ask him about it."

The bell rang, and the kids looked back toward

the town square. Even from this distance, they could see that Miss Calloway's posture was as stiff as ever.

Charlotte sighed. "Talking to Captain Ron will have to wait. For now, Miss Sunshine—I mean, Miss Calloway—calls."

CHAPTER EIGHT

ANOTHER FORGOTTEN LEGEND

Miss Calloway led the students to the steps of the jailhouse, where Sheriff Gordon was carving a small block of wood.

As the kids gathered around to watch the sheriff whittling, Miss Calloway turned to walk away. And when she passed by Stanley, he noticed something out of place. Her bonnet, dress, and white gloves were as starched and immaculate as ever, but the tips of her boots, poking out from under her dress, were covered in mud.

She walked to the post office, climbed halfway up the stairs, hesitated... then walked up the rest of the way and disappeared behind the door.

That was weird, Stanley thought.

He turned back to Sheriff Gordon, who had put away his whittling and was now spinning his six-shooters around on his fingers. With a flourish, he holstered them, and the kids clapped and called for more.

"More, huh?" Gordon said. "Watch this."

His guns were out of his holsters before anybody even saw his hands move. He spun them forward, backward, side to side, behind his back, and over his head. Finally, he tossed them both into the air, caught them by the handles, and holstered them by crossing his arms.

The kids roared with approval.

"You're the coolest person in the whole world!" Felix yelled.

The sheriff smoothed down his mustache. "You ain't seen nothin' yet."

He strode into the center of Main Street, stopped, and acted as though he were facing an imaginary person at the other end. He growled. "So it's come to this, has it, Smelly Bart?"

"I don't see anyone," whispered Gertie.

"I think he's pretending," Charlotte whispered back.

"Or he's a lunatic," said Herman.

Sheriff Gordon continued his show. "It's just you, the most dangerous outlaw in the land, versus me, America's sheriff," he shouted. "There's only room enough for one of us in these parts. I challenge you to a shootout. Winner stays in Forgotten. Loser goes home without dessert."

"Ouch," said Felix. "They're playing for keeps."

"Smelly Bart, I suggest you draw, if you ain't the yellow-bellied lizard I know you are. But before you do, get a load of this."

Sheriff Gordon drew out a whip. He flicked it to his left and his right, shattering glass jars that seemed to have been put there for just such an occasion. He flicked the whip behind him and smashed a third jar without even looking.

"And this!"

He flipped a large coin high into the air, shot at it, holstered his gun, and caught the coin with the same hand. He tossed it to a girl in the front row, and Stanley thought she was going to faint in admiration. She held up the coin, showing everyone the hole shot right through its center.

The kids went wild.

Sheriff Gordon tilted down the brim of his hat. "See, kids, being a lawman can be cool."

"It's cool, I'll grant you that," said Gina Von Grubin, who was perhaps the only kid who didn't seem that impressed. "But can you please explain to us what an Old West sheriff is doing in 1800s West

Virginia coal country?"

"Well, well, well," Gordon said. "A fellow history buff in our midst. Yes, I admit that of all the people who live in this town year round, I'm probably the most out of place, historically. As a matter of fact, I *was* a sheriff at an Old West town in Colorado until a couple years ago. Hence that display you just witnessed. But when I read about an opening here for a professional with my particular set of skills, I knew it was too big an opportunity to pass up. I mean, what better way to be remembered than to end up in Forgotten?"

Sheriff Gordon smiled, clearly very pleased with himself.

As Gordon talked, Stanley turned to look back at the post office once more. He was still wondering about Miss Calloway's behavior. Through the window, he could see Miss Nellie seated behind the counter. Miss Calloway stood in front of her, pointing outside and talking. They both seemed animated. Stanley wished he were the one who was talking with Miss Nellie. If he could just ask her some questions about her locket, maybe he could get the clue he needed.

The sheriff was still talking. "Mining towns like Forgotten only came into existence because of the coal. Before someone in the early 1800s decided to dig out the coal under your feet, this was just another small part of a big forest. And even after the mining started, a lot of towns like this never grew to house more than a few dozen people. Since townspeople had to pay for their own law enforcement, most small towns didn't even hire real sheriffs. If they had a problem, they just dealt with it themselves."

Gina raised her hand. "But didn't a lack of official law enforcement lead to a lot of vigilante justice?"

"Sometimes it did," Gordon said. "But for the most part small towns like this only had real problems was when someone came upon a 'bonanza.'"

"*Bonanza*," Felix said. "That's my grandpa's favorite TV show. Funny, I never saw the episode about Forgotten."

"No," Gordon said. "Not *Bonanza* the TV show, though I do identify pretty heavily with Little Joe. Bonanza was a term people used when someone found valuable ore, something much more valuable than coal. Diamonds, gems, silver, gold. That kind of thing. As a matter of fact, for hardworking coal miners, the absolute *worst* thing they could hear was some fool screaming they'd found gold in them hills."

"I don't get it," Gertie said. "Why would finding diamonds or gold be a bad thing?"

"Because even the rumor of something that valuable makes people go crazy," Gordon said. "Take gold, for instance. It ain't like coal. It's not found in a nice fat seam that goes miles and miles. Gold is incredibly rare and spreads through rock like tiny fingers. Even the biggest gold booms only last a short period of time before all the deposit's been found. But since you don't need much gold to make you filthy rich, the very rumor of gold dust will bring prospectors from all of the country like *that*." Gordon snapped his fingers. "The whole countryside goes crazy with prospectors before any one person can claim their rightful gold. That's why if you're smart, you don't want a gold rumor starting."

The sheriff drew his index finger over his curly mustache and looked thoughtfully at the kids. He leaned his head toward them and dropped his voice to a whisper. "I like you kids, so I'm going to tell you something about this town that most people don't believe ever happened. There's a legend that goes as far back as old guys have told—"

Felix jumped up. "Is it the Legend of the Red Canary?"

"No, it is not the Legend of the Red Canary."

Felix jumped up again. "No Head Fred?"

"No," Sheriff Gordon said. "It's not the Legend of No Head Fred either. I'm talking about the Legend of Forgotten's Gold. The story is that a long, long time ago there was gold found in the Forgotten mines."

"Gold?" Stanley asked. "In Forgotten?"

Gordon nodded. "But apparently, the people who found it were smart, and they kept their discovery all quiet-like. They mined only a little of the gold, and they took it out east. And they told no one. Because they knew if word got out, the rest of the gold would be gone like *that*." Gordon snapped his fingers again.

"So when did they come back and get the rest of the gold?" Staley asked.

Sheriff Gordon shook his head. "No one knows why, but they never came back. And for the last century and a half, bold adventurers have chased the tale of Forgotten gold."

"Do you believe the story?" Stanley asked.

Sheriff Gordon looked him in the eye. "Son, only a fool would believe that story."

"Sheriff Gordon," a voice snapped from behind them.

Stanley turned to see Miss Calloway. If possible, she looked more perturbed than normal.

"Shouldn't you be showing them the jailhouse?" Miss Calloway said.

"Yes, of course, Miss Calloway." Sheriff Gordon tipped the front of his cowboy hat. "Kids, if you'll just follow me into my office here, I'll show you a few tools of the trade."

The kids shuffled inside. It wasn't a big place—just a single room with a desk for the sheriff, with two jail cells next to it—and everyone had to pack in like sardines.

"This looks just like the old cowboy movies," Felix said. He peered through the bars of one of the cells. "Beds look cozy. Think they'll let me sleep here tonight?"

"Hey, Sheriff," barked Dervin. "Has anybody ever broken out of your jail before?"

The sheriff shook the bars of one of the jail cells. "Impossible."

Herman gave Stanley a curious look. "Nothing's impossible."

"Any questions, kids?" Sheriff Gordon asked.

"I have one," Felix said. "A certain friend of mine is convinced that you have suspicious rumblings in this town, and I've got to be honest, even I can hear some kind of a humming sound. What's up with that?"

"A rumbling?" Gordon shrugged. "I suppose the only thing that would explain a strange rumbling would have something to do with... an ancient dragon and a certain headless ghost who calls Forgotten home."

"Really?" said Stanley.

Sheriff Gordon nodded solemnly.

Stanley tried not to let that thought freak him out. He had an investigation to pursue. "Sheriff," he said, his voice a bit shaky, "how do you find time to do all the things you need to around here?"

Gordon pulled a pocket organizer from his leather vest. "With this little baby. She runs my life. For instance, on Mondays I typically—"

Stanley interrupted. "Let's take Miss Nellie's missing locket, for instance. What sort of investigation have you done on that?"

Sheriff Gordon looked a bit uneasy. "Um, well, I went after the culprit," he said.

"And did you find him?" Stanley asked.

"Not exactly."

"What did you do to follow up?"

Sheriff Gordon said nothing.

"That sweet old lady—" Stanley started.

"Is *old*," Gordon finished. "You'll understand when you grow up. But sometimes when people reach her age... well, they think things happen that don't. And they can't remember what happened five minutes ago. My guess is Miss Nellie lost that locket a long time ago. She just forgets from time to time."

Charlotte shook her head in disbelief. "You're saying she just made up that story about someone ripping a locket off her neck?"

"I believe *you're* the one who just said that," said Gordon.

"Would it kill you to do some investigating?" Gertie said. "What proof do you have that it wasn't stolen?"

"What proof do you have that it was?" Gordon said. His smile was gone.

"Would it interest you to know that several small items were stolen on the train ride here yesterday?" Charlotte said.

Stanley had noticed Polly snaking her way through the crowd, but at Gertie's comment, she stopped. And she smiled. Like she knew something.

"And it was only minutes after we got to town that Miss Nellie's locket went missing," Herman added.

The sheriff plopped down in his chair and plunked his cowboy boots onto the corner of his desk. "That is interesting, and maybe even a little suspicious," he said. "You may be on to something." He stroked his mustache and appeared to be in thought. When he looked up at the students, he startled, as if he'd forgotten they were there. "I'll take it under consideration."

The bell rang, and Miss Calloway's shouted from outside, "Time to visit the blacksmith!"

But as everyone started to file out of the sheriff's office, Stanley thought of one last question.

"Sheriff Gordon, have you ever seen Miss Nellie's locket?"

He shrugged. "Sure."

"Have you ever seen the inside of her locket?"

"Inside? One time, I think."

"What was in it?"

Sheriff Gordon scratched at his head. "A bird. A little tiny bird."

CHAPTER NINE

THE CHALLENGE

His full name was Robert Bob, but everybody called him Bob Bob Blacksmith. He was a tall man with a thick chest and forearms that would make Popeye jealous. He wore a thick leather apron and had goggles hung around his neck.

"They've even written nursery rhymes about me," he was saying. "Bob Bob Blacksmith, have you any coal? Yes sir, yes sir, three bags full."

Bob showed the kids how to fashion a double-sided axe handle in the forge by pounding the hot metal with his blacksmith tools. It was really cool to see how he worked the metal, but the smithy was way too hot for Stanley, so he was glad when the dinner bell rang.

Besides, he had a question for Bob. He waited until the other kids had hustled off to dinner.

"Bob Bob?" he said.

"You can just call me Bob," said the blacksmith.

"Okay, Bob. Did you hear that Miss Nellie's locket was stolen?"

Bob frowned. "Yes, I did. Now who would do such a thing to a kind old woman?" He shook his head.

"Is the locket valuable?"

Bob looked surprised. "I can't imagine it would be. But I can tell you this: it was worth a lot to Miss Nellie."

"I heard there's a picture of a little bird inside."

"That's right," said Bob. "It's a canary. I saw it about six months ago, when she asked me to fix the chain on the locket."

"Why does she have a picture of a canary in a locket?" Stanley asked.

Bob shrugged. "I don't know exactly. Canaries used to detect fatal gas leaks in mines. If you came from a mining family, wouldn't they mean a lot to you? And besides, it wasn't just a picture."

"What do you mean?"

Bob grimaced like he was thinking hard. "Well, let's see... There was a picture of a canary inside a circle. And connecting the bird to the circle was a line. And there was a number on the line."

At the sound of a number, Stanley's ears really perked up. "I don't suppose you remember that number, do you?"

"Sure. One hundred."

"Are you sure?"

"Of course I'm sure. Like I said, it was weird. And that's not all."

"There's more?"

"Another number. Right next to the bird. A little tiny 45."

Stanley shook his head. "Forty-five. You're sure about that?"

"That mean something to you?"

Stanley smiled. Not exactly. At least, not yet. But circles and numbers? He could do something with that. "I just like numbers. Thank you so much!"

Stanley started toward the door, excited to share this information with his friends, when Blacksmith Bob hollered at him.

"Hey kid, there was one more thing. That canary?"

"Yeah?"

"It was red."

Felix was weeping again when Stanley arrived at the Math Inspectors' table with his tray of food.

Stanley sighed. "Should I ask, or do I just ignore him like usual?"

"It's just... these are the best tacos I've ever had in my life," Felix said. "And to think, I'm not going to eat any of Slimy Sam's food after this week. It's just so cruel!"

Herman leaned in toward Gertie. "I could paint him blue tonight if you'd like."

Gertie actually seemed to consider it. Then she shook her head. "Nah, I've got other ways to handle him." She punched Felix really hard in the shoulder.

Stanley sat down and told the other Math Inspectors everything he'd learned talking with Sheriff Gordon and Bob Bob Blacksmith.

"A canary?" Charlotte said.

"A *red* canary," he replied.

"So kind of like the Legend of the Red Canary?" asked Felix.

Stanley shrugged. "Weird, huh?"

Herman grabbed Gertie's notebook and pulled a pencil out of his pocket. "Think you could describe it again?"

Stanley described what Bob had told him once more, and Herman drew a picture to match. When he was finished, everybody looked at it.

Felix shook his head. "I definitely do not get it."

Stanley grabbed the drawing. "Then I say we go ask Nellie about it."

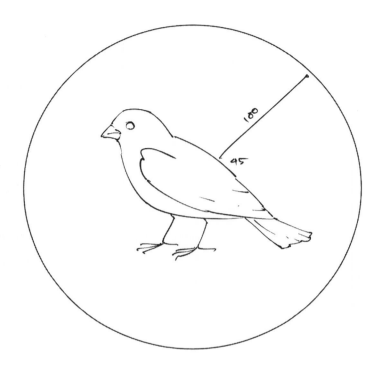

As soon as dinner was over, the Math Inspectors walked over to the post office. Stanley knocked on the door and waited.

There was no answer.

He knocked again.

"The light's not on, Stanley," said Charlotte. "I don't think she's home."

"Where's an old lady like her going to be this time of night?"

"Anywhere she pleases," a stern voice said behind them.

Stanley wheeled around. Miss Calloway stood at the bottom of the steps, hands on her hips, looking as delightful as always.

"Just what do you kids think you're doing?" she said.

"We wanted to speak with Miss Nellie."

"Leave that poor woman alone. Now, I think I made it clear that after dinner you children were to retire to your bunkhouses. Lights off at nine. Until then, you can visit, you can play cards, or you can read. What you *cannot* do is wander around Forgotten. Now, lest you get lost on the way, I'm happy to accompany you."

That night, Stanley was awoken by a whisper.

He opened his eyes. The moon was shining through the window, and he saw that Herman or Felix had pulled the dresser away from the secret door in the wall. The door was open—and Gertie was poking her head in.

"We've solved the mystery of the locket!" she said.

Stanley sat up. "You have?"

"Yes, but you have to come outside so we can explain it."

Stanley gulped. "Right now?"

"No, Stanley, next year. Of *course* right now."

Stanley felt himself shaking, but he slipped on his jeans and shoes. Felix went through the secret door first, and Stanley took a deep breath and followed. Herman came last, pulling the dresser into place behind them.

Charlotte and Gertie were both waiting outside. Charlotte held a small battery-powered lantern that illuminated their faces.

"Okay," said Stanley. "What did you figure out?"

Gertie motioned with her hand. "We'll have more privacy over here."

They followed Gertie up the rocky path. It felt to Stanley like they were already far enough from the bunkhouse that nobody would hear them, but Gertie kept going.

She led them over a small ridge, and that's when Stanley stopped. He couldn't believe his eyes.

"What is *she* doing here?" he said with a shaking voice.

"I don't like it any more than you do, Stanley," said Polly, who was clearly waiting for them to arrive. As usual, she was flanked by the English Club creeps.

"Gertie, Charlotte?" Stanley said. "Explain."

"Stanley," said Charlotte. "Gertie wasn't entirely truthful with you back there."

"Actually," Gertie said, "I wasn't even *remotely* truthful with you back there. I told you we'd solved the locket case in order to get you out here."

"You *lied* to us?" Felix said.

Gertie smiled. "I tricked you in pursuit of the greater good."

Charlotte shook her head. "You see, Polly and Gertie got into it at our bunkhouse, and one thing led to another, and before I knew it they'd both double-dog dared each other to go search the mine to prove that there is no such thing as No Head Fred."

"Why would you do that?" Stanley asked Gertie.

Charlotte grabbed Stanley's arm and squeezed. "Polly *challenged* us," she whispered. "And I know you don't like it, but sometimes it's best to face your fears. So this is what we're going to do, and you're not going to be scared, and we're going to get through it just fine because like I keep telling you—"

"There's no such thing as ghosts," Stanley whispered.

Charlotte smiled and let go of his arm.

Gertie turned to Polly. "Okay, English dweebs. Lead the way."

For the first time in their young lives, the Math Inspectors and the English Club were doing something together. On purpose. Of course, it was only to prove who was the most scared of ghosts.

Stanley already knew the answer to that question. *Him*. And it wasn't even close.

As they got closer to the cave, he tried to control his breathing and remind himself there was no such thing as ghosts. But all he could think about was the humming sound. And it was getting louder.

They stopped at the mouth of the cave. A blast of cool air hit them, as it had earlier in the day.

Polly pointed her flashlight beam into the darkness. "Last chance to chicken out," she said. "I know how protective you all are of little Stanley."

Charlotte lifted her lantern. "Stanley's our leader," she said. "He'll walk into that cave like it's his own house."

Stanley thought of a dozen places he'd rather walk into, and none of them were pleasant. But every member of the English Club and the Math Inspectors was looking at him.

He closed his eyes and stepped into the cave.

Herman slipped in after him. Polly came next, with Charlotte right behind her. Gertie and Felix and the English Club all squished in behind.

Herman pulled a small flashlight from his pocket. "Don't worry," he whispered to Stanley. "I'll stay right with you. Remember, I'm really good at stuff like this. You have nothing to worry about."

Stanley had to admit, being with Herman did make him feel a little better. But only a little.

They walked deeper into the dark and cool cave. Herman kept the flashlight beam in front of them, and every once in a while he would whisper to Stanley, "One foot in front of the other, nice and easy." And the farther they went, the more comfortable Stanley became.

The mine was basically a large tunnel, with lots of smaller tunnels branching off from it on both sides. Stanley couldn't help but think how easy it would be to get lost in here, under the mountain. He was glad they stayed close to the little train track that ran right down the center of the main tunnel. That must be for the Little Rascal—the train Felix would get to drive tomorrow.

Polly shoved past Stanley. "This is taking forever," she said. "We're taking over."

The rest of the group went on by, leaving Stanley and Herman bringing up the rear. As Gertie passed, she hissed, "Speed up, guys. You're making us look bad."

Herman pulled the flashlight beam back so that it lit up his own face. "Don't listen to them, Stanley," he said with a smile. "We'll go at whatever pace you want. You're doing great."

Stanley was just about to say thank you when something caught his eye. He pointed down. "Herman, look at that."

Herman shone his flashlight on the floor. "Cool bird."

"Not just a bird," Stanley said. "It's a canary."

Stanley bent down to get a closer look. It was incredible. Somebody had painstakingly embedded small rocks into the cave floor, like a mosaic, to form a picture. A picture of a canary.

"What's a picture of a canary doing on the cave floor?" Herman asked.

"I have no earthly idea," said Stanley.

Screams rang out from the tunnel ahead of them.

Herman swung the flashlight in that direction. The rest of the kids were running back up the tunnel toward them. All of them were screaming.

"Run for your life!" Felix shouted.

Herman's flashlight illuminated the scene. Felix, Gertie, Charlotte, Polly, and the English Club were sprinting, screaming, and clearly terrified.

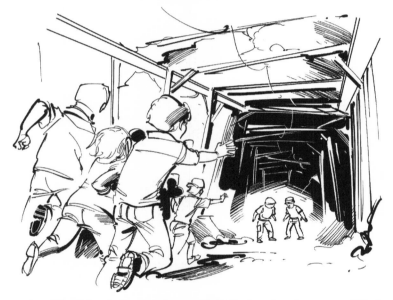

And behind them, just visible in the beam of light, was another figure. It was chasing them.

And it had no head.

Stanley wanted to run—he wanted to run more than anything. But he was frozen, unable to move. His heart pounded in his chest. His body shook with fear.

Thankfully, Herman grabbed him by the collar and jerked him away, and Stanley's feet started moving as fast as his heart.

The kids sprinted back to the cave entrance as fast as they could. When they hit the outdoors, they didn't stop, or even slow down. They ran straight down the rocky path to the bunkhouses. And without saying a word, the girls went to their bunkhouse and the boys to theirs.

Stanley's body was shaking worse than it ever had in his life. He curled up in the corner against his backpack and closed his eyes. But all he could picture was the image of the headless man running. And all he could hear was the pounding of his own heart, and the relentless humming of Forgotten.

CHAPTER TEN

CASE SOLVED

The next morning, Stanley came to a decision.

He had faced No Head Fred in a dark and spooky mine, and he was alive to tell the tale. He felt brave.

Okay, maybe not *brave* exactly. But definitely not terrified out of his mind. And for Stanley Robinson Carusoe, that was a start.

As long as he didn't have to take a dark and spooky stroll through that mine again.

He knew there was no such thing as ghosts. But between the missing locket, the headless figure, and that relentless humming, there *was* a mystery here—and he was determined to solve it. He couldn't stop thinking about the canary picture he and Herman had seen on the cave floor. There had to be a connection between that image and the stolen locket. So he slipped out of the bunkhouse before anyone else and headed for the post office to talk to Miss Nellie.

As he walked across the town square, a yawning Mayor Goatcheese was coming toward him. He was in his pinstriped suit with top hat and pocket watch. He smiled and waved.

And that's when Stanley noticed something. He stopped and stared.

"What you looking at, kid?" the mayor asked.

Stanley pointed. "You've got mud on your shoes."

Mayor Goatcheese stopped. He looked at Stanley strangely. Then he pointed at Stanley's feet. "You've got mud on *your* shoes. Fun game. Sorry, kid, I'm too tired this morning. I need some delicious Slimy Sam breakfast sausage." He walked off toward the mess hall.

Stanley's looked at the dry and dusty dirt streets of Forgotten, and his thoughts raced.

He ran up the steps to the post office and banged on the door. At the moment, he didn't really care about knocking so early in the morning. He needed answers.

He waited a minute, then banged on the door again. The lights were off, but he kept on banging.

"Why are you banging on Miss Nellie's door so early in the morning?"

Stanley turned to see the conductor, Captain Ron. "I have to ask Miss Nellie a question," he explained. "Do you know where she might be?"

"Nellie? Never can tell with her. Sometimes she wanders off."

Captain Ron started to walk off, but Stanley wasn't going to let this chance slip away.

"Excuse me, Captain Ron, could I ask you a question?"

Captain Ron stopped and shrugged. Stanley instinctively examined the man's boots. The tops were clean, but just around the edges at the bottom, there was an outline of dried mud.

"Why did you pull the emergency brake to stop the train when we came into Forgotten?" Stanley asked.

Captain Ron's eye twitched. "Why are you asking?"

"Because I want to know why an experienced engineer like yourself would put a trainload of kids at jeopardy by pulling an emergency brake when he had plenty of time to slow the train down and bring it to a controlled stop."

"I don't know what you're talking about."

Stanley stepped toward him. "I think you do, sir."

"*I* think I don't have time for your silly questions, and I think you need to get some breakfast in your system. Good day." Captain Ron walked off.

Stanley sat down on the steps in front of the post

office, trying to piece it together. But his thoughts were swirling. There was too much information—or not enough.

Bob Bob Blacksmith came out of his shop and stretched his arms. As he started walking toward the mess hall, Stanley checked out his boots. They were clean. No mud at all.

"Mr. Bob?" Stanley called, jogging over to him.

The tall blacksmith stopped and smiled. "Let me guess, more questions."

"Just one. When was the last time you went into the mine?"

"That's easy: never. I've never gone inside the mine. I'm claustrophobic, so me and mines don't mix. Marv wanted to give me the grand tour one time, but I didn't see the point."

"Okay. Thanks, Bob."

Bob smiled and strode toward the mess hall.

Stanley was hungry enough to follow, but he had something else he needed to do first. He circled the town square, observing the activity—and the shoes.

Sheriff Gordon came out of his office. His boots were clean as a whistle.

Sally the seamstress stepped outside to sweep up. Her shoes were clean, too. Sally's sister, Betty the butter churner, walked past. Clean shoes as well.

And then Miss Calloway showed up. As usual, she did not look happy. And just like yesterday, she had mud on her shoes.

"You," she snapped, pointing at Stanley. "Why aren't you with the other kids?"

"Why do you have mud on your shoes?" Stanley asked.

For a moment, Miss Calloway look surprised. Then she regained her composure, and her expression hardened. "You'll join the other kids, or I will make today *very* miserable for you." She marched Stanley to the mess hall.

Stanley filled a tray and joined the Math Inspectors for breakfast. They were unusually quiet. Even Felix was subdued, which was weird, considering Slimy Sam's breakfast sausage was delicious, and he had four of the sausage links sticking out of his mouth.

For once, Stanley was the only one *not* scared out of his mind. He cleared his throat. "Are you all still freaked out by the—"

"The headless ghost that chased us out of the mine last night?" said Gertie. "Yeah, pretty much. Aren't you?"

"Oh, yeah, I've never been more scared in my life. Until I remembered: there's no such things as ghosts. Plus, even if there were, they only come out at night, and it's daytime. So let's get investigating."

"Listen up!" Coach Carter bellowed from the front of the mess hall. Miss Calloway was next to him, and Polly stood beside her, grinning from ear to ear.

"Students, we have a bit of a situation," Miss Calloway said. "You will all exit the mess hall and go to the mine a little early. Marv is waiting for you there. He will get you started with your morning lesson."

As everybody stood to leave, Miss Calloway, Coach Carter, and Polly made a beeline for the Math Inspectors. "Not you," Miss Calloway said to the Math Inspectors. "You kids are coming with me."

She marched them to the boys' bunkhouse and ushered them all inside, including the girls. Coach Carter and Polly came along, too.

Miss Calloway turned to Polly. "Okay, young lady, tell us what you told Coach Carter."

Polly looked solemn. "As you may know, my detective agency has been investigating Miss Nellie's missing locket. My investigation led me to believe that whoever stole the locket also stole Gina's watch and my bracelet. After a couple days, my investigation led to one suspect, and one suspect only."

With a smile, Polly pointed.

At Herman.

"And so, this morning, I waited until the boys left their bunkhouse, then I slipped inside and found Herman's backpack. And in addition to finding a large roll of duct tape, I found these!"

Polly pulled her hand from behind her back. In it were a bracelet and a watch with a broken face.

Herman jumped up in the air. "She's a liar! Those were never in my bag!"

Polly advanced toward him. "Oh, so you were hiding the loot someplace else and *then* put it in your bag?"

"That's not what he's saying at all," said Felix.

"But I hope this doesn't mean you'll never go out with me."

"I'm saying I never stole those things!" Herman insisted.

Miss Calloway hand her hands on her hips. "Then how do you explain them being in your bag?"

"They *weren't* in my bag! They were probably behind her back this whole time!"

Miss Calloway scratched her chin. "Why would this young lady say they were in your bag if they weren't?"

Gertie jumped in. "Because she's evil! And worse, she loves English! Need I say more?"

Charlotte put a hand on Gertie's arm. "Miss Calloway, there's no way you can be certain whether Polly is telling the truth or whether she's lying in order to get Herman in trouble. But I'll give you a little hint: she's lying to get Herman in trouble."

"I am not lying!" Polly shrieked. She looked up at Coach Carter for help, but he didn't say anything.

Miss Calloway sighed. "I'm afraid I don't have enough information to act," she said. "Young lady, if you had your suspicions, you should have alerted me first. Then *I* could have looked in his bag. As it is, we really can't be certain who's telling the truth." She shook her head. "You kids have one full day left here in Forgotten. I suggest you behave, because I *will* be watching you." She turned to Polly. "*All* of you."

Miss Calloway, Polly, and Coach Carter left the bunkhouse. And just as they were walking through the door, Stanley noticed it.

Coach Carter's shoes.

They were covered in mud.

CHAPTER ELEVEN

A QUESTION OF KILOWATTS

By the time the Math Inspectors arrived at the entrance to the mine, the rest of their classmates were already wearing mining caps, and Marv was showing them how to use a pickaxe.

"Glad you could join us," said Marv. He passed mining caps to Stanley and his friends, then smiled at Felix. "Ready for the Little Rascal, you big rascal?"

Felix beamed. "Just bring her out here, and I'll show them all how it's done."

"That's the spirit. The Little Rascal is just inside the mine. Let's go take her for a ride."

Marv started into the mine, and everyone followed. Everyone, that is, except for the Math Inspectors and the English Club, who stood nervously at the entrance.

"Is there a problem?" Marv asked, looking back at them.

"I hate mines," Polly said. "You can bring the coal to me if you want, but I am not going in there."

"Same here," said Gertie, then shook her head. "Wait—did I just agree with Polly? On second thought, I'm coming with you, Marv. Better the ghost you don't know than the ghoul you do. Come on, Felix, you want to drive the train or not?"

Soon the Math Inspectors were following Gertie down the mine's main tunnel after their classmates.

"If it's ghosts you're worried about," Marv said, "don't. They never attack when there's this many people. Just don't get left behind."

The kids took his advice and stuck close to the group. There was comfort in numbers, and Stanley felt better by holding on to one thought: there was a problem to be solved.

So as the class walked forward, their way lit by the lights on their mining caps, and as Marv talked on and on about sedimentary rocks and different kinds of mining, Stanley kept his eye out. He wanted to see that canary picture again.

It was right where he remembered it.

Stanley stopped in front of it, and as the rest of the class continued down the tunnel with Marv, the Math Inspectors gathered around him. With their headlamps providing illumination, Stanley scanned the floor for clues. But he couldn't find any. He shook his head in frustration.

"So, a canary, right in the middle of the cave floor," said Gertie. "What's it mean?"

Stanley frowned. "I have no idea."

"Hey, kids!" Marv yelled. "Better keep up or you're gonna get left behind!"

They quickly caught up with the others.

The kids spent the whole morning in the mine, learning how to get coal and rock out from the wall. Learning how to fill up a coal cart. And learning how to pull the coal cart should a mule not be available. Deeper inside the mine, Marv showed them the heavy wooden doors that controlled air flow. And he showed them where a nipper sat, ready to open the doors for the mules. If the previous day's lesson on breaker boys and girls didn't convince the seventh graders of Ravensburg that mining was not fun, this did the trick.

The only upside was that the more time they spent in the mines, the more convinced they were of their safety.

Finally, they walked to the Little Rascal, which was parked on one of the occasional circular turnarounds they'd seen along the main tunnel. Marv led Felix to the steam engine and spent ten minutes going over every button and every lever, telling Felix what to do and in precisely which order. Every time he asked Felix if he understood, Felix just mumbled "uh-huh" with an expression on his face somewhere between happy and clueless.

Finally, Marv nodded to Felix.

Felix jumped into the little seat, his long legs and knobby knees packed into the scrunched little space, and started flipping levers and turning knobs like mad.

Marv yelled "No!" But before he could do anything, the Little Rascal let out a puff of thick black smoke, a blast of steam, and then... nothing.

Shaking his head, Marv went over the instructions with Felix one more time. When he was certain Felix could do it right, he gave him a thumbs up... and asked all of the children to stand back.

"Actually," he said, "stand *way* back."

Felix's second attempt didn't go any better than the first. In fact, this time was even worse. Hot steam hissed out of the engine, thick black smoke filled the cave, and Marv yelled for everybody to run.

They raced out of the cave as fast as they could. Marv and Felix were the last ones out. Their faces were black with soot and ash. Felix was trembling.

"I thought you understood how to do it," Marv said.

"I thought I did too," said Felix.

"So what happened?"

"To be perfectly honest, I wasn't really listening to you. I figured a kid who's been driving model trains his whole life should be able to just sort of drive any train."

Marv looked like he was about to lose it, but just then the lunch bell rang, and the kids scampered off back to town. All except for Stanley, who stayed behind with an angry Marv.

An awkward silence filled the air.

Actually, it wasn't quite silent. There was that humming. It was particularly loud here, near the mine.

"Marv," Stanley said, I've got a question."

"Will it really annoy me?" Marv asked, apparently still fuming about Felix's failure.

"I hope not. Can you tell me what that humming sound is?"

Marv smiled. "The humming?"

"Yes." Stanley's voice squeaked.

Marv's eyes twinkled. "Come on. Follow me, and I'll show you."

Marv led Stanley to the other side of the barn where Stanley half-expected Marv to throw him into the giant belly of a prehistoric beast. Over here, the humming grew to a ferocious roar, and Stanley was tempted to run for his life. But Marv led him not to a beast, but to an enormous metal machine that was coughing and burping out smoke.

"So it's not a dragon!" Stanley said.

"Nope," said Marv. "This is our two-thousand-kilowatt diesel generator. It's a real beast. Not the kind of beast they tell stories about, but a beast nonetheless. This is how we provide electricity to Forgotten."

Stanley relaxed. "That's a lot better than a dragon."

Marv laughed and slapped him on the back.

Stanley had one other question. "Marv, have they ever found gold in these hills?"

Marv's face twisted. "Gold? In these hills?" He looked at Stanley strangely, then shook his head. "No gold around these parts. This here's coal country."

It was Slimy Sam's Ooey Gooey Cheese Day at the mess hall. She'd prepared macaroni and cheese, grilled cheese, fried cheese balls, and a picture booth where people took pictures saying "Cheese!" All the cheese was a good thing, because it distracted Felix from his epic humiliation upon the Little Rascal.

The Math Inspectors spent most of lunch talking about what the canary figure on the cave floor might mean, what the numbers 100 and 45 referred to, and what, if anything, Nellie's locket had to do with it all.

Then Stanley told them he'd solved the mystery of the humming. "It's a diesel generator. A two-thousand-kilowatt diesel generator. Marv called it a real beast."

Felix stopped eating his grilled cheese sandwich mid-bite, the cheese hanging from his bottom lip. "That doesn't make any sense. Are you sure it wasn't a two-*hundred*-kilowatt generator?"

"I'm sure," Stanley said. "That's what Marv said, and it was labeled in big letters right across the front. Two thousand kilowatts. Why?"

Felix put down his sandwich. "Because it's the wrong size. By a lot."

"What are you talking about?" Gertie asked.

"Remember, Stanley, when we did that project on how to size a generator for our homes?"

"Of course."

"We had to look at our electric bills and figure out what was the average amount of kilowatt-hours used per month. Then we had to figure out what was the month with the highest number of kilowatt-hours used. *Then* we had to factor in what would be the highest time of electricity usage during a particular day. Based on that information, we came up with the right size generator for our home."

"What are you getting at?" Charlotte asked.

"A two-thousand-watt generator is way, *way* too big for a town as small as Forgotten."

CHAPTER TWELVE

THE TEXT MESSAGE

"What's it mean?" asked Gertie.

"It means they're producing way more electricity than a little town like this would ever need," said Felix.

"Maybe they're just wasteful?" Charlotte suggested.

Stanley thought. "Or maybe they're using the electricity for something else."

"Like what?"

"I noticed that humming on the first night we were here. They run that generator all night. Which is weird, because the lights go off at nine p.m. and the town stays dark. What are they using it for? And more to the point, why so much?"

"Are you having another Stanley?" Charlotte asked.

Stanley shrugged. "I guess I am. I've been paying attention to the adults. And... I think they're hiding something. And I'm beginning to suspect it has something to do with the mines."

"Can any of this help prove that I didn't steal that jewelry?" Herman asked.

Stanley had almost forgotten about Herman's troubles. "Yeah, about that. I need to have a little chat with someone. But first, we've got to find Miss Nellie."

The bell rang, and Miss Calloway and Coach Carter appeared at the front of the mess hall. Coach Carter slapped his hands together. "Today we've got a great surprise. We're going to play a rousing game of Capture the Flag. Bus your trays and move out!"

Coach Carter and Miss Calloway split the seventh grade into two teams. One team included the English Club, along with Dervin and his goons. The other team included the Math Inspectors and the Science Club.

"It's like she split us into good versus evil," Gertie said.

Charlotte looked over at the Science Club, which was now practicing a "flag-capturing celebration" with Felix. It apparently involved lots of elbows and knees and people falling down. She shook her head. "More like *goofy* versus evil."

Then Miss Calloway stepped forward to explain the rules. "Capture the Flag was a very different and much longer game in the 1800s," she began. "A typical match is best out of seven. Whoever wins four first, or has the most wins at the end of five hours, will be your winner."

"Five *hours*? Is she joking?" Gertie said. "I get tired after playing three rounds of rock-paper-scissors."

Herman eyed the stern, buttoned-up teacher. "I don't think Miss Calloway is capable of joking."

But Stanley knew what was going on. This was the 1800s equivalent of putting in a long movie when you got tired of teaching. Miss Calloway was just trying to keep them busy.

And Stanley thought he knew why. According to the schedule, they were supposed to spend time at the post office with Miss Nellie. Apparently, Miss Calloway didn't want that to happen.

"I think Miss Nellie is gone," Stanley said.

"What do you mean, gone?" asked Charlotte.

"I mean missing. Oh, they say she's a nice old lady who likes to wander off, but I'm not buying it. I think she's really and truly missing. And they don't know why."

"Okay," said Charlotte. "Stanley, I want you to work the problem. Don't even worry about playing Capture the Flag. Just wander around the grass and use that noodle of yours." She tightened her hands into fists. "I'll take care of the game."

The marathon Capture the Flag match was just that: a marathon. But Stanley spent the whole time wandering around the playing field, lost in his thoughts. This was a puzzle, and he was close to the solution. He just knew it.

After the sixth game, he noticed Polly on the sidelines looking supremely bored. He walked over to her.

"Polly," he said, "I'm coming in peace, and I need to ask you something. This isn't about war or anything like that. You've accused a good friend of mine of a crime. That's really, really serious. And I want to know: why are you making up a story about finding the jewelry in his backpack?"

Polly was cleaning her boots with one of her friend's tee shirts. She looked up at Stanley with a sneer. "I told the truth, Stanley. I opened Herman's backpack and that stuff was there."

Stanley had had a lot of encounters with Polly through the years. She was mean and spiteful, and sometimes even dishonest. But at the moment, she didn't seem like she was lying.

"Fine," said Stanley. "You said your investigation led you to his backpack. How, exactly?"

At this, Polly's expression changed. It was no longer a sneer. This was the Polly's "hiding something" face.

"I used brilliant deductive reasoning," she said.

"Based on what evidence?"

"Why should I tell you?"

Stanley stepped closer to her and growled. "Tell me the evidence that led you to Herman!"

Polly rolled her eyes. "It wasn't exactly evidence, okay? I got a tip. A reliable source said he had strong suspicions of Herman and suggested I look in his backpack."

"A reliable source?" Stanley said. "Who?"

Polly crossed her arms and tilted her head to one side. "I do not rat on fellow poets, Stanley. Plus, he swore me to secrecy. And now, this conversation is over."

Stanley started to say something more, then noticed what Polly had been cleaning off her boots.

Mud.

He looked out to where the kids were playing Capture the Flag. Lots of grass. Lots of dirt. Plenty of dust.

But no mud.

A series of pictures flashed into Stanley's mind. The train. The first day in Forgotten. Miss Nellie's stolen locket. The canary on the cave floor . His chance meeting with Captain Rob. The generator. Polly's "reliable source."

Then he looked down at his own shoes... and all of a sudden everything started to fall into place.

He spun around. Miss Calloway and Coach Carter were standing off to one side, watching the game. Marv was sitting on a grassy hill by himself. Mayor Goatcheese was pacing back and forth like he'd bet some money on the match. Sheriff Gordon looked like he was just arriving from his office. And away from all of them, near the train depot, was Captain Ron.

Stanley had confronted the train engineer directly last time, and that hadn't worked so well. Time to take a different approach.

He strolled casually over to the man. "Captain Ron, could I ask you a favor?"

Ron folded his arms. "You gonna be asking me weird questions like you did the last time?"

"No, not at all. Sorry about that. It's something else. I noticed you have a cell phone, and I know we're not supposed to... Well... the thing is... my aunt is really sick, and I'm worried about her. If I could just send my mom a quick text asking how she is, I would really, really appreciate it."

"Your aunt, eh?"

"We're close."

"Well, you'll be back home soon. I'm sure your aunt will be just fine for a few more days."

"She's really sick with—with something horrible," Stanley said.

Captain Ron's mouth twisted. Then finally, he took a breath and handed over the phone. "Just don't take too long. And for goodness' sakes, don't download any games. You kids and your new-fangled games!"

"Thanks, Captain Ron."

Stanley grabbed Captain Ron's phone. And while he *pretended* to send a text to his mom's cell number, what he was *actually* doing was looking for any texts Captain Ron had received on the day they'd arrived in Forgotten. Specifically, any text that had come in around the time they first arrived in town.

"Well?" said Captain Ron.

Stanley looked up. "My mom's slow at texting. Just give me a minute."

He found the text he was looking for. It was an inbound text coming from a number he didn't recognize, arriving at 7:14 p.m. And it said something odd and cryptic.

"You'll help me or I swear, I'll finally reveal your creepy past."

Stanley's heart almost stopped.

"Everything okay, kid?"

Stanley stared at the text for another moment. A long moment. And then he quickly sent a new text message to Felix's phone number just in case Captain Ron checked. *"Will Aunty be okay?"*

Then he handed Ron the phone. "Looks like my mom's not near her phone. Maybe if she texts back you can let me know. Thanks, Captain Ron."

Ron gave him a funny look, then climbed aboard the Commodore Golden Wing.

Stanley turned back to the game. The English Club was holding the final flag, and Charlotte and Gertie were kicking the air in frustration. And Stanley? He was trying to move the pieces around in his mind. He thought about all the different people in Forgotten. About who might have stolen

Nellie's locket. Who might have framed Herman for stealing the bracelet and watch. What the extra electricity was for. And why some of the adults in town had mud on their boots.

Things were starting to take shape. It wasn't a perfect fit at all, but Stanley was beginning to wonder if this mystery even *had* a perfect fit.

As he watched Polly and the English Club celebrate their victory, Stanley told himself that it didn't really matter who won the battle, it only mattered who won the war. And sometimes, he reminded himself, the field of battle didn't have a perfect solution. Sometimes, war required a calculated risk.

He crossed the field and walked up to Sheriff Gordon, who was busy with his whittling. "Sheriff," Stanley said in his most polite voice. "Would you be willing to do something for me?"

"Sorry, kid," the sheriff said. "I've already promised this carved mule to that tall goofy redheaded kid out there."

"It's not that," Stanley said. "I've solved the case of Miss Nellie's missing locket. I know who stole it."

"Sure you did, sonny," said the sheriff. "Sure you did."

"I also know where Miss Nellie is."

Sheriff Gordon's knife stopped mid stroke, and

his head jerked up. He fixed Stanley with a steely stare. "What do you mean?"

"I know who kidnapped her," Stanley said.

"Kidnapped?" Gordon looked around quickly to make sure nobody else was listening. Then he leaned in and whispered, "Okay, kid, I'll listen to you. But we need to wait till everyone else is in bed for the night. When all your friends have gone to the bunkhouses after dinner, you come talk to me at the jail."

"Fine," Stanley said. "But I need you to gather up a few people for me." He told the sheriff who he wanted to be there.

Sheriff Gordon ran a hand across his chin, then blew out a long, purposeful breath. "Okay, let's see what you can do. And kid? I don't like looking foolish... so you'd better get this right."

As Sheriff Gordon walked away, Stanley turned and joined a disappointed Herman.

"I didn't think I could lose at Capture the Flag to a bunch of English snobs," Herman said, "but I kept tripping over members of the Science Club."

"Forget about that, Herman, I've got something more important."

"Should I get the others?"

Stanley smiled. "No, Herman, this is a special mission, just for you."

CHAPTER THIRTEEN

STANLEY HAS A HUNCH

The Math Inspectors had already sat down with their food when Herman ran into the mess hall and walked straight over to Stanley.

"How on earth did you know that would be there?" Herman whispered. He opened his hand to show Stanley something.

"Wow," said Stanley. "I guess you'd call it a..."

"Stanley," Herman said, smiling.

Gertie cleared her throat. "Mind telling the rest of us what this is all about?"

Stanley grabbed the little treasure from Herman, put it in a paper napkin, and then set it on the table.

Everyone leaned in.

"A little piece of glass?" Gertie said.

Stanley smiled. "I'd better start at the beginning."

And so he did. He laid out all the facts, the things that didn't add up, and a whole lot of guesses. And then he told them about the meeting after dinner in the sheriff's office.

Charlotte frowned. "But Stanley, this is the farthest thing from an airtight case. Are you sure we should do this?"

"I'm sure of one thing. Miss Nellie's locket was stolen and now she's missing. Something is going on. And before anything bad happens to her, I want Sheriff Gordon to at least know what's been going on. And remember, this is Forgotten, the town of scary ghost stories."

"What's that got to do with anything?" asked Felix.

Stanley smiled. "Because if we get lucky, then maybe, just maybe, our villain will get spooked. But Herman, I do have one last thing for you to do."

Felix insisted on triple helpings of Slimy Sam's going-away dessert, and he would have gone in for a fourth helping had the bell not sounded an end to mealtime. While the rest of the class filed down the dirt road to the bunkhouses, the Math Inspectors slipped into the shadow of the jail building. They waited until the town was quiet, then went inside.

The sheriff's office was empty, but soon sounds on the stairs outside told them their company had arrived.

Sheriff Gordon entered with Mayor Goatcheese, Marv, Miss Calloway, Coach Carter, and Captain Ron. Miss Calloway's arms were crossed, and she looked even more unpleasant than normal, if that was possible.

"Sheriff Gordon," she said, "what's the emergency worth bringing us all here after dark?"

Coach Carter stepped forward and pointed to the Math Inspectors. "And what are my students doing here?"

The sheriff held up his hands. "Everybody, just relax. These kids are the reason you're here. They claim to have solved an important case."

Miss Calloway scowled. "This is nonsense. I'm leaving."

"No, you're not," Gordon said. "We're all staying until we get to the bottom of this."

"Where's Nellie?" asked Captain Ron.

Sheriff Gordon shook his head. "Still couldn't find her." He turned to Stanley and gave him a slight nod. "Son, you best get started."

Stanley cleared his throat. "Not long after we arrived in Forgotten, Miss Nellie's locket was stolen right off of her neck. I asked myself: Who would do such a thing? And more importantly, why?"

Miss Calloway pointed at Herman. "I believe you have your prime suspect right there in this boy, seeing as he was found with two other pieces of stolen jewelry. And if you try my patience much longer, I may just revisit my decision not to punish him for that crime—and perhaps the theft of Nellie's locket, too."

"First of all," said Stanley, "his name is Herman Dale. Second of all, he didn't steal the jewelry on the train. And he didn't steal Nellie's locket." Stanley and Herman exchanged a mischievous smile. "But he *did* steal something. At least, hopefully."

"What?" Sheriff Gordon asked.

Stanley pushed his glasses up the bridge of his

nose. "We'll get to that later. But first, a story. One day, my mom and I were going into a little shop—"

Mayor Goatcheese rolled his eyes. "I don't have time for this."

"Really, Mayor Goatcheese?" said Stanley. "Do you have someplace you need to go at this time of night?"

The mayor shifted uncomfortably. "Well, no."

"Good. Now, as I was saying. One day, my mom and I were going into a little shop on Ravensburg's Main Street. My mom went in first, and as the door swung back, a gust of wind blew it right into my knee. It really hurt. And it made me so mad that I did something very unusual for me. I kicked as hard as I could at the big window next to the door. And I cracked it from the very bottom all the way to the top. I got into a lot of trouble that day."

"Thrilling," Miss Calloway said. "What's your point?"

"My point is, sometimes when people are angry, they do things they normally wouldn't do. And sometimes when people get scared, they do the same thing."

"Sounds like the beginning of an accusation," said Marv.

"It's more like a line of questioning," Stanley said.

"And what's your question?"

Stanley turned to Captain Ron. "I've asked you this before, but now I'll ask in front of all these witnesses. Why did you pull the emergency brake the day we arrived?"

Captain Ron threw up his hands. "This again? There were mules on the track! Mules!"

Stanley looked the engineer in the eyes. "Are you sure you want to go with that answer?"

Captain Ron hesitated. "Of course I'm sure," he snapped. "I'm a decorated veteran of the railway. I know my stuff. What do you kids know about anything?"

"We know what happened. You pulled the brake on the train, and the train stopped. Then we climbed out of the train and walked. We walked about a quarter of a mile to the train depot."

"So what?"

"So what?" asked Gertie. "Do you know how short my legs are?"

"Actually," said Stanley, "as short as Gertie's legs are, that wasn't really our biggest concern. You see our big goofy friend Felix here? He's smart. Really smart. He told us that a train that small, going that slow, would have no problem coming to a stop in a half mile. Which means..."

Captain Ron's face suddenly changed. He was nervous.

"Which means you didn't have to slam on that brake to stop the train," Stanley continued. "You had plenty of track for a normal stop. The mules were a nice excuse, but you didn't pull the emergency brake because of those mules. You're hiding something, Captain Ron. What is it?"

Captain Ron looked at the floor and put his head in his hands. He didn't say a word.

"I don't follow," said Marv. "What exactly have you just proven?"

"Just one piece of the puzzle," Stanley said. "Felix, tell Marv about another one."

"There's a humming sound in Forgotten," Felix said. "A dragon in the mines, right? Sounds reasonable, and at first I bought into it. But it turns out the source of the humming isn't a donut-craving dragon, and it has nothing to do with No Head Fred. The source of all the humming in Forgotten is a diesel generator. I think you can all agree that this is a very small town. And you yourself, Marv, told us the mine is no longer operational, other than the little bit of mining you do for the education of your junior coal miners."

It was Marv's turn to shift uncomfortably. "So?"

"I've done the math," Felix said. "Turns out, for a town this size, the biggest generator you'd need would be about three hundred kilowatts. And yet, right behind your barn, there's a two-*thousand*-kilowatt generator. Which raises the question: What do you need all that electricity for? And why does it run all through the night?"

"And..." Stanley added, "what are you hiding, Marv?"

Like Ron, Marv didn't answer.

"This is a complete waste of time," said Miss Calloway. "I've got better things to do."

"I know you do," Stanley said. "I first noticed you were up to something the day we toured this jailhouse. You came to pick us up, Miss Calloway, dressed as perfectly as always. Clean, buttoned up, immaculate. Except for the mud on your shoes. Not dirt, mind you, but *mud*. Mayor Goatcheese told us himself: this has been the driest six weeks Forgotten's had in memory. The whole town is nothing but dust. In fact, the only mud around here is found in only one place. Want to tell us what you're hiding, Miss Calloway?"

Miss Calloway didn't look away. She simply smiled and said, "Why don't you tell us another thrilling adventure from your childhood and find the answer there?"

"Instead of a story," Stanley said, "how about a legend? And instead of one, I've got two."

Miss Calloway's smile faltered.

Charlotte spoke next. "The first legend comes from the early 1800s," she said. "The legend says that around that time, gold was discovered in Forgotten. But the discoverers thought it was best to leave most of it and come back when they could plan a quiet excavation. However—or so goes the legend—those discoverers never came back. And that's why fortune hunters have come to Forgotten ever since in search of the legendary gold."

Charlotte looked at Stanley, who nodded for her to continue.

"The second legend is about a headless ghost named No Head Fred," she said. "He patrols the Forgotten mines at night. It's a pretty convenient way to keep competition away, don't you think?"

"Thank you, Charlotte," said Stanley. "So—how do the mud and the legends fit together? That clicked when I noticed that Marv's boots had mud on them just like Miss Calloway's shoes did. And where did Marv's mud come from? From inside the *mines*. The mines are the only source of mud in Forgotten during this dry spell. So I took the liberty of observing the shoes of all the adults in Forgotten.

And do you know whose boots *don't* have mud on them? Just five people." He counted off on his fingers. "Slimy Sam. Blacksmith Bob. Sally the Seamstress. Betty the Butter Churner. And Sheriff Gordon."

Stanley took a long moment to let the meaning of his words settle over the room.

No one said a word.

"Fine," Stanley said. "If none of you want to share anything, then allow Gertie to."

Gertie stepped forward. "Once Stanley figured out the mud came from the mines, other things started to make sense. That's the reason for all the electricity. It's being used in the mines. Because the people of Forgotten—specifically, most of the people in this room—spend their nights, every night as near as we can tell, mining... and looking for the Forgotten gold."

The adults all looked at each other as if they didn't quite know what to do next.

Mayor Goatcheese in particular seemed rather annoyed that their little secret had been finally exposed. "You think you're pretty smart, don't you?" he said to Stanley.

Felix held up his finger. "Nope, I think I'm pretty smart. But my friend Stanley? He *knows* he's smart."

"Say that you're right," said the mayor. "Say that we are looking for gold. Last I checked, looking for gold wasn't a crime."

Stanley shrugged. "Maybe. But for something that's not a crime, you've gone to a lot of trouble to hide what you're doing, haven't you?"

Miss Calloway stepped forward. "Sheriff Gordon said you solved an important case!"

Stanley took a deep breath. This was the part that would be tricky. "Mayor Goatcheese is right. The fact that a bunch of you work at this educational town just so you can spend your nights looking for gold is sneaky... but it probably isn't a crime. Probably. But you know what *is* a crime? Stealing an old woman's locket off her neck. And you know what's an even *bigger* crime? Kidnapping that same woman."

The whole room let out a collective gasp.

Marv stepped forward. "You can't really think we would kidnap Nellie. Everyone loves her!"

"Did you love her enough to let her in on the secret that at night you go looking for gold?"

At that, Marv said nothing.

"Marv, if it makes you feel any better, I don't think you kidnapped Nellie. But the person who did kidnap Nellie is the same person who stole her locket!"

"I'll go back to what I said at the beginning," said Miss Calloway. She pointed at Herman. "*This boy* is the one who stole the locket. Are you saying this boy kidnapped Miss Nellie?"

"Again, his name is Herman. And Miss Calloway, you said it yourself. You didn't have enough evidence to prove that Herman really stole those things. You had the word of a girl named Polly, a girl who hates us, by the way. Now, I spoke with Polly about this matter earlier today. She insists that she really did find the bracelet and the watch in Herman's bag."

"And you believe her?" asked Marv.

"I do."

"Then I'm confused," said Mayor Goatcheese. "Doesn't that prove your friend stole the jewelry?"

"It only proves that somebody put the jewelry in his bag. And you know what else Polly told me? That she had a reliable source who told her where to look."

"Who?"

"She wouldn't say."

Miss Calloway growled. "Why are you speaking in riddles?"

"I don't mean to, honestly. But this mystery was tough to piece together. Polly didn't tell me exactly...

but she did give me a couple of clues. She said it was a 'he' and she said it was a fellow poet. A man who likes poetry. Whoever that describes, *he's* the real villain around here."

The adults all looked at one another suspiciously.

Stanley continued. "There is a man in our midst who is looking for Forgotten gold, and somehow he figured out that Miss Nellie's locket has something to do with finding the gold. That's why he stole the locket our first night here. And in case you're wondering, Herman was right next to me when that locket was stolen, so it couldn't be him."

Miss Calloway didn't look convinced.

"Nope," said Stanley, "a man stole that locket, and he's been using it to try and find the gold. But my guess is... he couldn't figure it out. And that's why he kidnapped Miss Nellie. He kidnapped her so that she could tell him how to use the locket to unlock the secret of Forgotten's gold."

Marv's eyes grew wide. "Are you telling me Nellie's locket is the key to figuring out where the gold is?"

"That's my guess. You know how people talk about the Legend of the Red Canary?"

"Yeah," said Marv. "It's a story that nobody knows. Only that it's important to Forgotten."

"It *is* important... but it's not a story."

"What do you mean?" Miss Calloway asked.

"The Legend of the Red Canary is a legend... like a *map* legend. Inside of Miss Nellie's locket is a red canary, along with a circle, a line, and some numbers."

Calloway turned towards Goatcheese, her eyes wide. "There's a mosaic picture of a canary on the floor of the mine's main tunnel!"

"We never knew what it was for," said Goatcheese.

Marv ran his hand through his hair. "I've tried to think if there was some connection between that image and the gold... but it never made any sense to me. I thought it was just a warning to miners to be careful down there."

"It wouldn't have made sense to anybody," said Stanley. "Unless they had the locket."

"So who did it?" Miss Calloway asked. "Who stole the locket?"

"The person who stole the locket is a man. A man who likes poetry. A man who stole Polly's bracelet and Gina's watch. Both of which were stolen... while we were still on the train."

"I don't understand," said Marv. "You're saying it *really was* your friend?"

Stanley smiled. "Not so much. An interesting

thing happened when Captain Ron abruptly pulled on the emergency brake. Everybody on the train fell down. And as I was getting up, I noticed somebody rubbing their leg. I didn't think much of it at the time. But later, I started to wonder."

"What?" asked Mayor Goatcheese. "Wonder what?"

"I wondered if that person was rubbing their leg because they'd just fallen down on jewelry. Stolen jewelry they'd been keeping in their pocket."

"That's quite a leap in logic, don't you think?" asked Miss Calloway.

"I agree. It's a hunch, a funny feeling. My friends, they like to call it a—"

"STANLEY!" the rest of the Math Inspectors said in unison.

"But the most interesting thing about this is Gina Von Grubin's watch. Her stolen watch. Gina was nice enough to give it to me tonight for a little demonstration." Stanley pulled the watch out of his pocket and lifted it up for everyone to see.

"You'll notice that this watch is broken. There's a little bit of glass missing from the watch face. But what's *most* interesting is the time on this watch. It's stuck on the time it was when the watch was broken. Now thankfully, my friend Gertie is very dramatic, and my friend Charlotte has a perfect memory. When we all fell down on the train, my friend Gertie said something dramatic... and she even remarked on what time it was. Charlotte, do you remember what Gertie said?"

Charlotte smiled. "I sure do. Gertie said, and I quote: 'Seven fifteen p.m. The time I was almost killed by donkeys.'"

"And Marv, can you tell us what time this broken watch says?"

Marv leaned in, then looked up in amazement. "Seven fifteen!"

"Lady and gentlemen of Forgotten, it's time to tell you what's been happening around here over the past few days. There *was* a man on that train. A man who likes poetry. This man stole two pieces of jewelry. When the train stopped suddenly, this man fell down, and the watch in his pocket broke, causing a little piece of glass to fall out and the time to be stuck. Now, my friend Herman did not steal this jewelry, but to be honest... Herman does have some sneaky skills. And so, earlier this evening, I asked him to go to this man's bunkhouse, find the pants he was wearing that night, and look in the right front pocket. And what did he find?"

Stanley took out the folded napkin from his

pocket. Inside the napkin was a little piece of glass. He picked it up delicately between his thumb and finger and held it up.

"This piece of glass was still in the right front pocket." He placed the glass into the face of the broken watch. "And as you can see, it's a perfect match."

The adults exchanged nervous looks.

Mayor Goatcheese rubbed his chin. "I'm sorry, son, but a lot of this so-called evidence seems pretty circumstantial to me. I don't see any smoking gun. For all we know, your friend Herman here really is the one who stole the jewelry—maybe he planted the piece of glass, too. All we have is your word that someone else planted the stolen jewelry in Herman's bag. And why would anyone do that?"

"Good question, Mayor. Why would anyone want to frame Herman for the thefts of the watch and bracelet? It's quite simple: our villain was trying to connect the thefts of the jewelry on the train with the theft of Miss Nellie's locket. He was trying to make us think Herman stole Miss Nellie's locket, too—so you wouldn't question it. So you wouldn't guess the real reason behind the theft. You'd never know that he, the real villain, stole the locket in order to find the gold. Because he knows the rest of you are looking for the gold, too. And guess what: he doesn't plan on sharing it."

Stanley pushed his glasses up the bridge of his nose. "And I'll admit: so far, I've presented a lot of pieces of a puzzle that don't fit together perfectly. I don't have a smoking gun. But thanks to Herman's sneakiness, I do have myself a phone."

Herman handed Stanley a phone—Captain Ron's phone. Stanley pulled up the text message Captain Ron had received at 7:14 p.m. on the day they arrived in Forgotten.

"Hey, that's my phone!' said Captain Ron.

"Sorry," said Stanley. "I said earlier that Herman did have to steal something, and this is what I meant. He took it out of your pocket a few minutes ago. But I need it for a little demonstration."

"Give me my phone back!" said Captain Ron.

Sheriff Gordon stopped him with his hand. "Ron, I want to see this demonstration. Stanley, go ahead."

"Thank you, Sheriff. I told you all at the beginning, that sometimes when we get angry enough, we can do foolish things. Well, Captain Ron here got angry, and he did something foolish. He got a text message at 7:14, and at 7:15, he pulled the emergency brake, even though he could have done a controlled stop. Why? Because he wanted to make everybody on the train fall down. Or... well, really, he wanted *one* person to fall. The man who made him angry. The man who sent him this text."

Stanley read the text message on Captain Ron's phone. *"You'll help me or I swear, I'll finally reveal your creepy past."*

Stanley looked up from the phone. "I don't know what Captain Ron's creepy past is, but *somebody* did. And that somebody needed Captain Ron's help so badly it was worth blackmailing him. And the text so angered Captain Ron that he lashed out."

"Who sent him that text?" Miss Calloway asked.

"Well..." said Stanley. "It wasn't any of us Ravensburg students, because none of us were allowed to bring cell phones on the trip. And I don't think it could have been most of you adults, because I haven't seen most of you with cell phones on this trip. In fact, I've only seen two cell phones on this trip. The first is Captain Ron's. The other?"

Stanley hesitated as he scanned the assembled adults. He had to admit, he was enjoying this moment.

"Can you tell us who the text was from, or can't you?" Sheriff Gordon asked.

Stanley grinned. "I can do better. I can *show* you."

He pushed a button on Captain Ron's phone. Almost immediately, a ringing sound came from someone's pocket.

The right front pocket of... Coach Carter.

CHAPTER FOURTEEN

LOCKS AND LOCKETS

Carter pulled his phone from his pocket and turned off the call. Then he smiled one of those evil genius kind of smiles as he put the phone back in his pocket. He started to clap.

"Not bad, Math Inspectors. Not bad at all."

"Then you admit it?" said Miss Calloway.

"Admit what exactly?" said Coach Carter. "Admit to looking for gold? Sure. Admit to being mad at Captain Ron? Right again."

"No," said Marv. "I think what she means is, do you admit to stealing Nellie's locket?"

"And," added Stanley, "do you admit to kidnapping her?"

Carter rubbed his chin, his eyes dancing around like he was doing some sort of calculation. Stanley knew this wasn't the type of evidence likely to convict somebody in a court of law. But it was probably enough for a proper investigation. And

Stanley was counting on Sheriff Gordon for some help.

"Sheriff," said Stanley. "Don't you think you should, you know…"

"Lock up Coach Carter?" asked the sheriff.

"Well, yes!" said Gertie.

Gordon bit his lip, then he and Coach Carter exchanged a curious look.

Coach Carter nodded. "I think the kid's right, Sheriff. Somebody's definitely got to get locked up today. It's just not going to be me."

Carter snatched the pistol out of Sheriff Gordon's holster and pointed it at the crowd. "I'm really tired of people getting in my way. So in a way, I guess these annoying kids have solved my problem. I need you all to get inside these jail cells, and I need you to do it now!"

Herman shrugged. "I don't think you'd use a gun on a bunch of kids."

Carter smiled and lowered the gun. "Maybe. But I doubt Sheriff Gordon would have any trouble using his whip. Show 'em, Sheriff!"

Gordon pulled out his whip and snapped it just a couple feet away from Herman, shattering a glass bottle. Miss Calloway and Felix both screamed.

"Sheriff Gordon!" Felix shrieked. "But I thought

you were America's sheriff!"

The sheriff smiled. "Try paying the bills being America's sheriff, sonny. Plus, the rest of us were never going to find gold... so when Carter here told me that Captain Ron backed out on his plan and he needed my help for a little backup, it sounded like easy money to me."

Then he cracked his whip again for good measure.

Coach Carter and Sheriff Gordon pushed the Math Inspectors into one jail cell and the adults into the other cell.

"Stanley," said Coach Carter. "I gotta say, when Sheriff Gordon told me you wanted to see everybody, I was intrigued. I also thought it was a great way to gather my opponents in one room. And now that I've got you all contained..."

He grabbed the whip from Gordon's hand and shoved the sheriff into the cell with the other adults. Then he slammed the jail door shut and locked it.

Sheriff Gordon launched himself at the bars. "Why, you no-good double-crossing—"

"I know, I know, I'm a total scoundrel. But, Sheriff, you've served your usefulness. I needed someone watching my back... and now that everybody's locked in jail, well..." Carter laughed. "All you'd do now is take some of my gold. And I can't have that."

Coach Carter walked over to the other cell and locked eyes with Stanley. "Pretty impressive, you putting everything together the way you did. If it makes a difference to you, I'd have to say that in my short teaching career, you've been my star student."

"You don't have to do this, Coach," Stanley said.

"That's what they always tell the bad guy at the end of the movie."

"So you admit you're the bad guy?"

"I'm definitely not the good guy."

As Carter turned to walk away, Stanley knew he had to do something. In books and movies, whenever the hero was running out of options, he tried to keep the bad guy talking. So that's what Stanley tried to do.

"How did you even learn about the gold in the first place?" he asked.

Carter hesitated, then wheeled around and smiled. He puffed out his chest and walked back toward the cells. "Interesting you should ask. I'm a bit of a historian and an adventurer. But by profession, I'm a treasure hunter. And a while back, I was hired to track down a trunk of gold that many people thought went down in a ship lost at sea. My employers thought otherwise. In my research, I came across an old diary that belonged to the man believed to be in possession of the gold. The man said he'd found the treasure in a place that had been 'Forgotten.' He claimed this treasure had cost a man his life, and he'd regretted it ever since. The thing is, he always capitalized Forgotten.

"Well, I never did trace the gold that was on the ship, but I eventually worked backwards to find where the gold came from in the first place. I even made a few trips here as a visitor, always wearing a different disguise. I got to know these people, though they never had any idea who I was. And I figured out that most of the town was here just to look for the treasure.

"But there was one woman who seemed less concerned about the treasure than anyone else. Miss Nellie. I got to talking to her, and she eventually showed me her locket. I recognized immediately that the canary in the locket was identical to the canary image on the floor of the mine, and I *knew* there was a connection. So I made plans to come back to Forgotten—with a new disguise. This time I'd be myself, and I'd be chaperoning a bunch of snot-nosed kids. Nobody would suspect a thing."

"Until we did," said Stanley.

Carter frowned. "Yes, until you did."

"So you stole Nellie's necklace?" Herman said. "And Polly's bracelet and Gina's watch?"

Carter threw his hands up in the air. "Haven't you been paying attention? Of course I did!"

"No, I've been paying attention. I just wanted it officially on the record so people would stop thinking I'm the guy who steals everything."

"Well..." said Charlotte. "You *did* steal Captain

Ron's phone just a little bit ago."

"Well, sure. Except for that," Herman said.

"And you snuck into Carter's bunkhouse and went through his stuff," added Felix.

"Okay, that too," said Herman. "But that's using my powers for good. That's totally different."

"So you're basically Robin Hood?" Gertie suggested.

Herman smiled. "Finally, someone gets me!"

Stanley had another question for Coach Carter. The most important question of all.

"Did you kidnap Miss Nellie?"

"Kidnap? That's such a harsh word, an ugly word. No, I did not kidnap her. Truth is, all I wanted was her locket. But that old woman got nosy. She came into the mine guessing that whoever had taken the locket was using it to find the gold. She found me, and that's when my plan changed. I no longer had the time to figure it out on my own. I had to... persuade her to help me find the gold."

"And did she?"

Carter shrugged. "With enough persuasion, people will tell you anything."

"Did you hurt her?" Charlotte asked.

Carter frowned. "I would never hurt an old lady. But I did let her know that we'd be sitting alone in that mine for a very, very long time if she didn't help me out. And when I said that, well... she wised up. She told me how to use the Legend of the Red Canary." Carter smiled. "And I found the gold."

At that, all of the adults rushed the bars of the jail cell. "You found it?" asked Marv. "You really found it?"

Carter's smile grew. "Oh, you bet I did. And let me tell you, it is beautiful. But there's not a lot of it. Oh, there's enough to make me plenty rich... but not enough for me to want to share. The only problem is, with nothing but a pickaxe, it'll take me a long time to get that gold out. I was fine with that at first—figured I'd take my time, hole up in the woods for a few weeks while I mined it, bit by bit. But now, with Miss Nellie just sitting there, I no longer have that kind of time. That's why I came back this afternoon, to tell Sheriff Gordon about the favor I needed. And as long as it's still where he said it would be..."

Carter opened the bottom right drawer of Sheriff Gordon's desk. He pulled out a wooden box and held it up. On its side was one word.

A very powerful word.

"Thanks for the dynamite, Sheriff," Coach Carter said. "I wouldn't have known where to find it in all of Marv's stuff."

"You're going to dynamite the gold out?" asked Marv.

"I've run out of time so, it's my only option."

"Wait," said Marv. "Just tell me, are you north of the main tunnel or south?"

"Now Marv... feels like it would be cheating if I told you."

Marv shook the prison bars. "Come on, Carter! North or south?"

Carter rolled his eyes. "South. Why?"

Marv shook his head furiously. "I'm begging you, do *not* dynamite anywhere south of the main tunnel. South of the tunnel's been mined out. It's nothing but a series of wormholes. I tried dynamite there one time, and I just narrowly escaped a cave-in. I'm telling you, don't do it. That part of the mine can't handle dynamite."

Carter laughed. "That's exactly the type of thing I would tell someone if I didn't want them to find the gold."

Marv lowered his voice "I'm begging you, Carter, don't do this. You and Miss Nellie won't make it out of there alive."

Carter smiled. "Marv, I appreciate the attempt but... I do believe you're bluffing." He opened the door, and the cool night air flooded into the sheriff's office. "Goodbye, citizens of Forgotten, and farewell!"

CHAPTER FIFTEEN

THE CANARY IN THE MINE

Felix shook the bars of the cell. "Stella! Stella Burger! Where are you when we need a good reporter?"

"He's lost it," said Gertie.

"We've got to stop Coach Carter," Charlotte said. "Miss Nellie's in real trouble."

"I know," said Stanley. Then he noticed Herman. He was... smiling. "Herman? What are you grinning about?"

Herman pulled something out of his pocket and held it up. It was long and metal and shaped a lot like a key. But it wasn't a key—it was a twisted piece of metal. "Ever since they found that jewelry in my bag, I knew it was just a matter of time before they threw me in the clink. I figured I'd be needing a way to break myself out of jail, so I took a fork from the mess hall and fashioned myself a key."

"Think it'll work?" Gertie asked.

"There's only one way to find out."

Herman squeezed his arm through the bars and carefully inserted his homemade key into the lock. He wiggled it back and forth for a full minute, concentrating hard. Then something clicked. Herman turned the fork-key, and the door swung open.

Felix grabbed him by the shoulders. "I'm just glad you're using your evil genius for good these days. Milkshake at Mable's when we get back—my treat!"

As the Math Inspectors walked out of their cell, Gertie looked over at the adults in the other cell. "I'm not sure any of them deserve to get out."

"I'm not sure either," said Stanley. "But we need their help if we're going to stop Carter."

"That's going to be a problem," Herman said. His key was still in the lock on the door, and he was jiggling it back and forth. "It's stuck."

"Stuck?" Miss Calloway shrieked. "Well, find some other way to get us out!"

"They don't have time," said Marv.

"Marv's right," said Captain Ron. "You kids have to stop Carter and save Nellie before he blows the mine and it's too late."

"How are we supposed to even *find* him?" Gertie asked.

"To find him, you just have to find the gold," Captain Ron said.

"But how?" Gertie said. "Carter isn't exactly going to leave a trail of neon signs pointing the way. None of us knows where the gold is, remember?"

"So what do we do?" Herman asked.

Charlotte shook her head. "If Marv's right, then whatever we do, we need to do it quick. Stanley, you said the Legend of the Red Canary is the key to unlocking the location of the gold. Do you think you can figure it out?"

"If you help me? Yes."

Marv faced the kids. "Take the Little Rascal. I was going to use her tonight, so she's already got hot coal in her and she's ready to go. You'll need her if you're going to haul Nellie out of there. And if there *is* a cave-in, she'll be your fastest way out." He shook his finger at Felix. "You've got somebody who knows how to drive her."

Felix's eyes widened. "Me? You can't *possibly* mean me."

"Felix, you're the only one who can do it."

"But you saw me earlier today. I can't do it. I can't!"

Captain Ron shot his hands out of the jail cell, grabbed Felix by the shirt, and pulled him against the bars so that his cheeks squeezed against the metal.

"Oww," Felix said.

"You can do it you, Felix, and you must. The whole town is counting on you."

"I can't—"

Captain Ron pulled Felix harder into the bars. "Yes, you can. I didn't tell you this, but as soon as I saw you, I knew you were a fellow train enthusiast."

"You did?"

"Of course. I could see the look in your eyes. You've got something in you, kid." He released Felix, stepped back, ripped something off his own shirt, and held it out to Felix.

"Golden wings!" Felix screamed.

"Yes, sir. These are the golden wings I earned after gaining the captainship of the Commodore Golden Wing." Captain Ron thrust his hands through the bars and pinned the wings to Felix's shirt. "And now, the Golden Wings are yours."

Felix looked down at the wings and beamed.

"Are you crying?" Gertie asked.

"Yes," sniffed Felix. "Because I've just fulfilled my life's destiny." He paused. "And also because Captain Ron just stuck me in the chest when he pinned the wings on."

The Math Inspectors sprinted the entire way to the mine. They were out of breath by the time they reached it, but they didn't have time to rest. They had a job to do.

Felix, captain of the Little Rascal, approached the engine with confidence. He sat in the driver's seat, twisted some knobs, and hit some buttons.

"You sure you got this?" Stanley asked.

Felix smiled. "All aboard!"

The others jumped in the little cars, and the Little Rascal lurched forward. It picked up speed quickly.

Gertie smiled. "Well, how about that? I think he's got it."

The trip into the mine went quickly aboard the train. Felix didn't slow down until Herman's flashlight beam showed the canary on the cave floor. While Felix steered the train into the little roundabout that allowed it to turn and face back toward the exit, the others hopped out and examined the mosaic figure on the cave floor.

Stanley pulled from out the crumpled piece of paper Herman had sketched for him.

He flattened it out and set it on the cave floor, right in the middle of the canary.

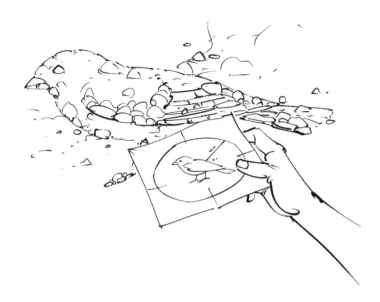

"Okay, if Bob Bob Blacksmith was right, then this is what the inside of Miss Nellie's locket looks like. A canary at the center of a circle. A radius line connecting the canary to the edge of the circle. The number 100 on the radius line. The number 45 next to the canary."

"So what does it all mean?" Herman asked.

Charlotte joined Stanley on the cave floor. She pointed to the line on the paper. "The simplest explanation is that to find the gold, you have to follow the direction of the line." She looked up and pointed in the direction of the line. "That way."

Gertie walked in the direction of Charlotte's

finger... right into a cave wall. "The only problem is this gigantic wall you run into. So unless you've got a tunnel boring machine in your back pocket, there's no way to follow the direction of the line."

Felix scratched at his chin. "Maybe, maybe not."

"What do you mean?" Stanley said.

"Maybe both Charlotte and Gertie are right. The number on the line says 100. So maybe to find the gold we need to go 100 feet. But Gertie's also right: it's not possible to walk through a stone wall. The question is, is there another way to get to the spot that is a hundred feet away in the same direction as this line?"

Stanley thought about it, and then it hit him.

"A unit circle!"

Felix smiled. "That's what I'm thinking."

Herman raised his hand. "Mind translating for the mathematically challenged kid with an affection for blue paint?"

"A unit circle is a circle with a radius of one," said Felix. "The circle in the locket has a radius of one hundred, but either way, it means the number next to the canary makes more sense. Forty-five probably refers to the angle of the line relative to a horizontal x-axis."

"Great," said Gertie. "Now we know the exact

angle of the direction we're supposed to travel from this canary in the cave floor. But that still brings us back to the problem of how we're going to tunnel through that wall."

Stanley smiled. "That's the beauty of the unit circle. Can I have your pencil again?"

Stanley grabbed Gertie's pencil and made a few new lines on the drawing of the locket.

"A triangle?" Herman asked.

"Sure. By drawing a line on the horizontal axis, and by dropping a line from the edge of the circle until it meets that line on the horizontal axis, we've now formed a triangle. But it's a very special triangle."

"A right triangle," said Charlotte.

"Why are we doing this?" asked Herman.

"Just wait, you'll see. What we really want to do is figure out the length of each of the sides of this right triangle. To do that, we need to use the Pythagorean theorem: $a^2 + b^2 = c^2$."

"The longest side in this picture is 100," Herman pointed out.

"We call that the hypotenuse. It's c in our equation."

"Okay..." said Herman. "How does this help?"

"Bear with us," said Charlotte. "We know that this is a right triangle, so this angle"—she pointed to the lower-right corner of the triangle—"is 90 degrees.

And we know this labled angle is 45 degrees..."

"Which means the third angle must also be 45 degrees, because thethree angles of any triangle add up to 180 degrees," said Gertie.

"Right," said Charlotte. "And if this triangle has two equal angles, then it also has to have two equal sides. It's isosceles."

"Which means," added Stanley, "that in this case, a=b. Putting that back into our equation, we have a^2 + a^2 = $(100)^2$."

He sketched out the math on the drawing:

$$2a^2 = 10,000$$
$$a^2 = 5000$$
$$a = \sqrt{5000}$$

"And," said Felix, "as everyone knows, the square root of 5000 is 70.71."

"I didn't know that," said Gertie.

"Me either," said Charlotte. "Stanley?"

"Afraid not," Stanley said. "But if Felix is correct—"

"I am," said Felix confidently.

"Then that means a = 70.71. Which means the two shorter sides of this triangle are both 70.71."

"Great," said Herman. "But back to my original

question: *Why are we doing this?"*

Stanley quickly labeled the triangle on the drawing. "Look at this piece of paper," he said to Herman.

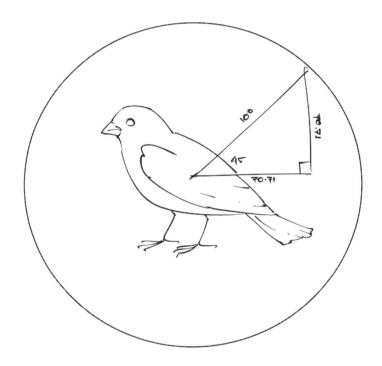

"In order to get from the middle of the circle to the point we've been talking about on the edge of the circle, you could travel on the hypotenuse line for 100 units. Or..." He stopped as he saw Herman trying to work it out.

All of a sudden, Herman's eyes lit up. He pointed

excitedly at the paper. "Or you could first travel horizontally along this short side of the triangle for 70.71 units, and then go straight up the other short side of the triangle another 70.71 units. That would also get you to that same spot on the circle."

"Exactly!" said Stanley. "We know that we can't travel at a 45-degree angle through that solid wall of rock." He grabbed Herman's flashlight and turned to his right. "But we *can* travel horizontally through this tunnel right here."

Felix stepped up beside them. "So, 70.71 units down this tunnel. Let's call it 71. The question, is 71 what?"

"Could be inches, feet, yards, miles," said Gertie.

"I'd say it's feet or yards," said Charlotte. "I doubt we'd have to walk miles, and inches would be silly."

"Which is it? Feet or yards?" Herman asked.

Stanley shrugged. "We might have to try both. So we'd better hurry."

They hustled into the tunnel that was perpendicular to the mine's main tunnel. They decided that was the most likely "x-axis." But keeping straight was tricky. The tunnels and shafts all twisted around, like giant worm holes, just like Marv had said. No wonder Nellie's great-grandfather had created himself a map.

Both Herman and Charlotte walked off the pace. When they made it to 71 feet, they stopped. There was a tunnel branching off to the left, just as they had hoped. But... they still weren't sure if "feet" was the right unit of measurement. It could be yards.

"I don't know," said Stanley. "We might need to split up. Three of us take this turn to the left, and the other two go farther until you make it to 71 yards."

"I think you should come this way," said a woman's voice.

Stanley jumped.

Herman shined his flashlight to the left, down the

branching tunnel. And there, maybe thirty feet away, tied to a chair, and looking tired and scared and very, very old... was Nellie.

CHAPTER SIXTEEN

TREASURE BEYOND MEASURE

"Nellie!" Stanley shouted.

They ran over, Herman untied her, and Stanley and Gertie helped her to her feet. She was a little wobbly, but otherwise seemed to be okay. In fact, there was a fire in her eyes that Stanley hadn't seen before.

"Carter's gone to set the dynamite," she said. "He's going to blow it to get at the gold. He'll bring this whole section of the mine down on top of us."

"That's what Marv told him," Herman said. "But he wouldn't listen."

Coach Carter stepped out of the shadows. He struck a match and lit a candle. The glow illuminated his face. It was dirty, sweaty, and determined. "So, the Math Inspectors found their way out of jail? Impressive. Most impressive. But I've come too far to have my gold taken from me by a gang of annoying kids."

"Who you calling annoying?" said Gertie. "Okay, Felix is annoying, I'll grant you that. And Herman's weird. I'd call the rest of us normal with a side of eccentric."

Herman leaned in toward Stanley. "Was Gertie just defending us or taking a shot at me? It's hard to tell sometimes."

"Enough!" Carter roared. "Do you have any idea how long I've been working for this? No. You don't. So you have no idea what I'm capable of. And trust me when I tell you this: I will not hesitate to hurt you if that's what I have to do."

Charlotte stepped toward him and puffed out her chest. "I'd like to see you try."

Carter's expression changed. It went from determined to... something else. His eyes grew bigger, angrier, crazier. He was a man who wanted gold. A man who'd do anything to get it.

Stanley was scared, but he stepped forward next to Charlotte.

Herman stepped up on her other side. Then Gertie joined them. Then Felix. And finally, Nellie.

For a terrible moment, they all stared at Coach Carter.

Then Carter started toward them.

"Stop it!" Miss Nellie screamed, and the command chased itself down the tunnel in a succession of echoes.

Carter stopped dead in his tracks.

"Just stop it!" she said. "I'm old and I'm tired. I'm so tired of gold, the endless search for gold, and what it makes people do. If you blow that dynamite, you'll get your gold, all right. It'll cover your grave for eternity. I don't care what your gut or your greed tell you. You don't know these caves like me, and like my family before me. Like my great-grandfather, Ricky Juneberry, who died because of that gold."

"Touching story, Nellie, but I've got work to do."

A ferocious growl came from Nellie's throat. "You will listen to me, Carter. Ricky Juneberry was an expert miner. A group of well-funded prospectors brought him in to look for the gold. And what do you know? They found it. They found gold. But these people my great-granddad worked for, they had a sickness. That sickness was *greed*. He got a bad feeling about what was going to happen. So he put that image of the canary in the floor as a marker for himself. Then he made the locket and gave it to his wife. But before he told her how to use the legend of the red canary, those greedy fools blew up the mine to hide their secret. But they forgot to tell Ricky. He died that day, buried in the explosion."

Carter's face, still illuminated by the candle in his hand, softened, and Stanley thought that maybe he was starting to have second thoughts.

"My great-grandpa was killed because of *gold*," Nellie continued. "And it didn't end with him, either. Over the years, my whole family caught gold fever. They roamed these caves trying to find it. It became an obsession—an obsession that made them waste the better years of their lives. It got me, too." She lowered her head. "I got the gold fever. I came searching too.

"But the difference is..." She looked up again. "I *found* the gold. I found the gold... and I let it be."

"But—why?" Carter asked. "Why wouldn't you take the gold for yourself?"

"And do what with it, young man? I had no family to share it with. I had nothing left to me but one thing: a mission. I could spare others the heartache of following an empty dream."

She stepped closer to Carter. "Don't do this. Gold isn't worth it. Take it from a very old lady who knows. No matter how much you find, it'll cost you everything."

Carter stayed silent for a long moment. Then he smiled. "That's a beautiful story, Miss Nellie. It really is. But unfortunately, I don't really care. I just want to be rich!"

He swiped his candle toward the ground. It ignited something at his feet.

A trail of black powder.

The black powder lit up like fireworks, and the flame raced like mad down the darkened tunnel.

"No!" Charlotte screamed.

She was about to race after the flame, but Stanley caught her arm. "There's no time! Everybody get back to the train! That's our only way out."

Herman and Gertie and Felix ran back the way they had come. Stanley and Charlotte grabbed Miss Nellie's arms. Then Stanley stopped.

"You go on ahead, Charlotte," he said. "Get Miss Nellie to safety."

"Why? What are you going to do?"

Stanley looked at Carter, who was just standing there watching the flame disappear into the darkness. "Just because Carter's a greedy creep, doesn't mean he deserves to die. Have Felix get that train moving as soon as you're there. We'll catch up."

Charlotte's gaze bored into Stanley.

"I promise," he said.

Without another word, Charlotte put Miss Nellie's arm over her shoulder and started back the way they came.

Stanley then turned to Carter. The man's focus was entirely on the disappearing flame—he wasn't worried about Stanley at all.

So Stanley did the only thing he could think of to get the man's attention.

He kicked him as hard as he could in the shin.

Carter screamed in pain. "What was that for?"

"Coach Carter, or whatever your name is, you're an amazing treasure hunter. How else could you have solved the puzzle? But I've got something you don't have. I get these funny feelings. My friends tease me about it all the time."

"Why are you telling me this?"

"Because I'm having one of those funny feelings right now. And it's telling me that as soon as that dynamite blows, this whole mine is going under. You won't make it, and neither will I. Don't be stupid. Don't lose your life over—"

A thunderous boom sounded from down the tunnel. Even though Stanley had known it was coming, the explosion still took him by surprise. He froze. So did Carter. And for a moment, everything in the cave seemed very still. Maybe everything would be okay. Maybe the mountain could handle it.

And then a rock fell from above them. And another. A rumble sounded from the direction of the explosion.

And Carter's eyes got as big as dinner plates. "Run!" he screamed.

With dust and dirt raining down, Carter and Stanley ran down the tunnel and took a right. They raced as fast as they could toward the main tunnel. Somewhere up ahead, the other Math Inspectors and Nellie were screaming for them to hurry. And Stanley did. In fact, he was quite certain he had never run so fast in his life. When a mine is falling apart all around you, it tends to give you an extra burst of speed. And when you're running for your life, 70.7 feet isn't really that far.

Just as Stanley and Carter dove into the Little Rascal, the branching tunnel behind them collapsed. It emitted a huge cloud of dust and debris that washed over the train.

And the main tunnel was shaking now, too.

"Go, Felix, go!" Gertie screamed.

The Little Rascal lurched forward, running fast and hot. Felix hunched over the controls, moving everything like an expert. He turned his hat backwards and pushed the train to its limits—like someone who had trains in his blood. Rocks from the ceiling hit the ground on both sides of them, and the train shook beneath them. It was like being in the middle of an earthquake and an avalanche all wrapped into one.

"Faster, Felix, Faster!" Herman screamed.

The mountain was coming apart at the seams, and all Stanley could do was pray. He prayed that he would make it out of this in one piece. That he would make it home to see his parents. That his friends, and Miss Nellie, and even Coach Carter, would be safe.

Then he heard something he didn't expect. From up ahead, he heard Felix shouting, "Yeee-hawwww!"

The little train shot out of the mouth of the mine just as an enormous cloud of dust exploded all around them.

The train took a sharp curve to the right and began to slow down. When it finally stopped, Stanley climbed out of the train and, along with Coach Carter, Nellie, and the others, stumbled as far from the mountain as he could. And when the dust finally settled and the glow from the moon allowed him to focus, he was astonished at what he saw.

The mouth to the cave was completely blocked with boulders and rocks.

The Forgotten mine was gone.

CHAPTER SEVENTEEN

THE RETURN OF NO HEAD FRED!

Mayor Goatcheese, Captain Ron, Miss Calloway, Marv, and even Sheriff Gordon were waiting for them outside the mine. Apparently, Bob Bob Blacksmith had heard screaming from the jail and had come over and opened the cell with an extra jail key that he had once fashioned for the sheriff. Sheriff Gordon asked all of them for forgiveness, and he promised to help them catch Carter.

And so it was that after the mine caved in, Sheriff Gordon and Mayor Goatcheese grabbed Carter and put some of Gordon's old handcuffs on him. Slimy Sam and Miss Calloway attended to Miss Nellie. And Captain Ron used his cell phone to call the authorities in the nearest town. Marv just sadly studied what used to be the mouth of the main cave but now looked like the side of any mountain.

All the kids were commended for their extraordinary bravery, and Felix was delighted when both Marv and Captain Ron congratulated him on his handling of the Little Rascal. Neither of them, they said, could have done any better. And everybody agreed that the way Stanley had been able to put the puzzle together was nothing short of brilliant.

All Stanley could do was shake his head bashfully and say, "I just had a funny feeling, that's all."

As the authorities dragged Coach Carter away, Stanley had to admit, he was pleased with how he'd been able to solve the puzzle. Math wasn't always just about numbers. Math, at its core, was a puzzle.

But there were a couple of things that he still didn't understand. And now seemed like the right time to clear them up.

"Captain Ron," he said, "I know this seems like a little thing, but there's something I still don't understand. Coach Gordon sent a text referring to your 'creepy' past. A text that made you awfully angry. I know it's none of my business, but—"

"So much wasted time," said Captain Ron. "That should be on my tombstone. So much wasted time. Listen, I did some stuff when I was young that I'm not proud of. Broke a few laws. It was wrong... but none of it was creepy. The reason I call it my creepy past actually has something to do with your little town of Ravensburg.

"You see, I was planning to leave the Northeast and head to Canada in order to lie low for a while. I needed money for the trip. I took this job, a modeling job, if you can believe it. Somebody at the old Hamilton Roller Coaster was putting in a new ride, Beepy the Clown, and they needed someone to be a model for this clown head that was supposed to go on the front of it. I had a big clown-like afro back in those days, so I did it. I made a few bucks and left the country. Years later, when I came back, I passed through Ravensburg and visited the Hamilton Amusement Park. That's when I saw the actual ride for the first time. By this time it was old and dilapidated, and that clown head was the scariest thing you ever did see. So everybody called it—"

"Creepy the Clown!" Felix shouted.

"You know it?"

Felix looked at Captain Ron like he was in the presence of greatness. "*You're* Creepy the Clown?" Felix began shaking in excitement.

"The big lug's going, Gertie," Charlotte warned.

"On it," said Gertie. She pulled a candy bar from

her pocket and shoved it into Felix's mouth. Then she gently helped him sit down.

"And that's why I refer to it as my 'Creepy' past."

"Captain Ron," said Stanley. "Everybody makes mistakes."

Miss Nellie spoke up. "And you refused to help Carter when it counted. That means something. It really does."

"There is one other thing I don't understand," said Stanley. "All those stories about No Head Fred? Well, the other night, we were scared away from the mine by an *actual* No Head Fred. My question is, just who is No Head Fred?"

The adults all looked at each other uncomfortably. Then finally, Mayor Goatcheese raised his hand. "I am No Head Fred."

"You?" said Stanley.

Captain Ron narrowed his eyes at the mayor. "What? No! *I* am No Head Fred."

Marv raised his hand. "Um, actually, *I* am No Head Fred."

"No, *I* am No Head Fred," Miss Calloway snapped.

Sheriff Gordon shook his head. "You're all wrong. *I* am no Head Fred."

The adults of Forgotten, West Virginia, were all claiming to be No Head Fred, the ghost that had terrified children for generations.

"I don't understand," said Stanley. "What's going on?"

The adults looked at each other uncomfortably again. When it appeared that Mayor Goatcheese was about to say something... one more adult raised her hand.

Nellie.

"I'm afraid they are all wrong," she said. "I am No Head Fred. I'm the *real* No Head Fred."

"You?"

"Yes, Stanley. Me. I told you that my great-granddad was buried alive in the mine before he could explain to his wife, my great-grandma, how to use the locket. Over time, every member of my family tried to find the gold. And so did I. And when I finally figured out the locket, I found the gold.

"But as soon as I found it, I realized I needed to keep that gold hidden. So I invented a ghost to scare people away. This was back when I was younger, of course, but I would occasionally pretend to be No Head Fred. It was fun. And it worked. Plus, it was a way—a strange way, I'll admit—to keep the legacy of my great-grandfather alive. People called him Ricky Juneberry, but his real name was Frederick Juneberry. Fred. So I kept him alive with the ghost,

No Head Fred. But also I named him that because of all the people who have lost their heads looking for gold."

She smiled. "And then these young whippersnappers came along and started looking for the gold, and *they* started to be No Head Fred, too. So I let them. And..." She smiled even wider and winked. "I also let them look for the gold—because I knew they weren't looking in the right place."

"Miss Nellie, how *could* you?" said Miss Calloway.

"Because I figured as long as you were looking for gold, you wouldn't leave. You would stay. My real family's been gone for a long time. And you all? You're my real family now. I didn't want you to leave. An old woman needs family."

For the first time, Stanley saw Miss Calloway relax. Her ramrod straight posture faded. She walked up to Nellie and gave her a hug. A long hug.

Finally, she backed up and wiped a tear from her cheek. "Maybe we could look for the gold together?"

Nellie looked at the mine, which had completely caved in. "I think that will take a long time."

Miss Calloway smiled. "Good. Because I'm not going anywhere."

Miss Nellie reached her hand into the pocket of her dress. She handed Miss Calloway a sucker and then took one for herself. "But first, let's have a lollipop. I do like my lollipops."

It was at that moment that Stanley heard more voices approaching. He turned to see the seventh-grade boys and girls, still in their pajamas, walking over the ridge toward the mine.

Polly Partridge, bleary-eyed and suddenly not so pretty, was in the lead. Her eyes got big as she surveyed the scene. "What on earth is going on here?"

Miss Calloway winked at Stanley and then walked right up to Polly. "Do you remember how you accused Herman of stealing that jewelry?"

"Well, yes. I solved the mystery."

Miss Calloway shook her head. "No, you did not solve the mystery. In fact, you could not have been more wrong. Turns out Coach Carter was the villain all along."

"He was?"

"And do you know who cracked the case?" asked Miss Calloway.

Polly's look of bewilderment suddenly melted into fear. Because it was at that moment that she saw Stanley Carusoe... and the smile plastered across his face.

"No," said Polly, shaking her head. "No!"

Miss Calloway nodded. "Yes, young lady, yes.

Turns out Stanley and his friends? They're the ones who actually solved the case."

Gertie smiled. "And trust me, Polly, I have the perfect public humiliation picked out just for you."

The look on Polly's face was priceless. And then she exploded and let out the loudest scream any of them had ever heard.

And in the spooky town of Forgotten, West Virginia, that was no small feat.

CHAPTER EIGHTEEN

MEANWHILE

A tall man with a thick chest and large forearms walked through the door of the little coffee shop and scanned the room. Next to the fireplace, a figure sat reading a book.

The tall man hesitated, then read the title of the book. *Macbeth*. He breathed a sigh of relief and walked over to the table.

"I didn't know if you'd meet me," he said, sliding heavily into a seat opposite the figure.

The figure didn't raise an eye from the book. "That's because it was stupid of you to come here."

"I was told—"

"You were told to stay put. And to watch. If you had something important to say, you should have written to the address we provided you."

"But this can't wait," said the tall man.

The figure continued to read, ignoring him.

"Fine, maybe I made a mistake," said the man.

Then he smiled. "Because maybe it doesn't matter that someone else knew about that gold in the 1800s."

The seated figure only flinched a little.

The tall man lowered his voice to a whisper. "And his name was Frederick Juneberry."

The figure at last closed the book and looked up into the eyes of the tall man. "You were right to come after all. That does indeed change things. This will be most interesting news to the Boss."

"Is there anything else you or the Boss would like me to do?"

The figure stood and studied the tall man. "Possibly. This new information might be what we need to complete our final act. But only the Boss knows that. The Boss knows everything."

The figure pulled an envelope out, dropped it on the table, and walked out of the coffee shop onto the busy streets of downtown Ravensburg, New York.

The tall man grabbed the envelope and greedily thumbed through the money. With this amount of cash, maybe he could finally find another line of work.

Maybe he'd finally worked his last day... as a blacksmith.

END OF BOOK FIVE

BONUS MATH PROBLEMS...

Do You Have What It Takes
To Be A Math Inspector?

GERTIE: *Hi there, math friends, it's me. But you already knew that, because this is the part of book you've all been waiting for...the math-in-action word problems! As ever, I'm joined by my lovely assistant Felix. Take it away, ya big lug.*

FELIX: *Well, we just went on our big seventh-grade fieldtrip to the old mining town of Forgotten, West Virginia. As you all know, because you're in my fan club, we used some crazy math skills to multiply justice and square root bad guys. But what you may not know is that while we were there, Gertie and I added to our history skills too. Specifically, we did a little behind-the-scenes research about what kids did for fun back in the old days. The first thing you should know is that almost none of them had smart phones.*

GERTIE: *What Felix is trying to say is that we've got a big project for history class that's due pretty soon, and we chose to research what sort of games kids played in the 1800s. There were tons, so we picked our favorites. And do you know why they're our favorites?*

FELIX: *I was hoping it was because they all involved eating as much old-fashioned apple pie as possible in the shortest amount of time.*

GERTIE: *Well, they don't. In fact, they all involve math. You all can give them a try and see what you think. All of these games can be played with four or more people, so get some friends and let's get going. As always, check your answers on our website TheMathInspectors.com.*

Game 1— Math Buzz

GERTIE: *Ok, I'll be "it" first. That means you all have to sit in a circle and I'll sit in the middle of the circle. Now I have to think of a sequence that forms a number pattern, but I won't tell anybody what it is.*

Once I'm ready, I'll point to a person in the circle who will say the number "one." The person to their right says the number "two," and so on around the circle.

When someone says one of the numbers in my secret sequence, I'll say the word "buzz." You all need to concentrate on which numbers get buzzed and try to figure out what the sequence is. If you do, then they raise your hand. If you can correctly explain the sequence to the group, you are awarded a point, and you get to sit in the middle of the circle and think of a sequence for everybody else to figure out.

Let's do a practice round: one, two (buzz), three, four (buzz), five, six (buzz), can you guess the sequence? That's right, the sequence is: Even numbers beginning with two.

Here's a harder one: one (buzz), two, three, four (buzz), five, six, seven,(buzz) eight, nine, ten (buzz), eleven, twelve, thirteen,(buzz)...

Word Problem # 1 – Can you guess what number will be buzzed next?

Word Problem # 2 – What's the sequence?

That was just practice. Now choose who will be "it" and play your own game until someone reaches 3 points. And if you are doing these problems by yourself, make up your own number sequence on a piece of scratch paper.

Game 2— Hunt the Shoe

FELIX: OK, my turn. You guys are going to love this game. I'll have you all stay in the same circle you were in for the last game, but this time I'll be in the middle. I'm going to hand one of my boots to one of you, and then I'll cover my hands with my eyes. I'll give you all 30 seconds to pass the shoe around the circle, but make sure to keep it behind your backs at all times. Then I'll open my eyes. I get to ask three questions, and you can only answer me "Yes" or "No." then I have to guess where the shoe is. Any questions?

GERTIE: I have two. First, are you crazy? Felix, this is the dumbest game I've ever heard of. No, not because you're having them pass around a boot. Because you're having them pass around your boot. By the smell of that thing, it's not going to take the person in the middle more than 2 seconds to sniff out its location. Secondly, what in the world does this have to do with math?

FELIX: Good point on my boot being a dead giveaway, Short Stuff. Let's use your shoes instead. But as to what this game has to do with math... it's all about the strategy. Take these next problems for example:

Word Problem # 3 – If there are 9 kids in the circle, what are my chances of finding the shoe in one guess?

Word Problem # 4 – If I use his three questions to figure out that three of you are not holding the shoe, what are my chances of finding the shoe then?

Game 3— Sack Race

GERTIE: *Let's talk sack races. You've probably seen this one before, because we still play it these days. It's pretty simple. You each get in a big sack, line up on the start line, and race to see who can jump to the finish line the fastest. So far, this might not seem like this is a math game. But like Felix said, it's all about the strategy. Take a look.*

Word Problem # 5 –Let's say the racecourse is 60 feet long, and Felix is foolish enough to challenge me to a sack race. Felix has those long skinny legs, so he jumps his sack 5 feet-per-jump and it takes him 2 seconds to complete each jump. I have somewhat smaller legs, so I jump my sack 3 feet-per-jump but I jump at a rate of 1 seconds-per-jump. If Felix and I competed in a sack race, which of us would cross the finish line first? How fast did Felix complete the race? How fast did I complete the race?

Game 4— Able-Whackets

FELIX: *This last game is the greatest thing I ever heard of, and yes, it's actually a real game people used to play. The greatest thing about it is this— nobody knows anything about the real rules except that the loser is whacked hard over the knuckles with a tightly wound handkerchief. Who wants to play?*

GERTIE: *Well, I was wrong about the boot game, Felix. This one is the dumbest game I've ever heard of.*

Well, thanks for playing with us today, and wish us luck on our project!
Gertie and Felix out

DID YOU ENJOY THIS BOOK? CAN YOU PLEASE LEAVE A SHORT REVIEW?

HONEST REVIEWS OF MY BOOKS HELP BRING THEM TO THE ATTENTION OF OTHER READERS. IF YOU'VE ENJOYED THIS BOOK, I'D BE VERY GRATEFUL IF YOU COULD SPEND JUST FIVE MINUTES LEAVING A REVIEW (IT CAN BE AS SHORT AS YOU LIKE) ON THE BOOK'S AMAZON PAGE.

THANK YOU VERY MUCH!

THE MATH INSPECTORS BOOKS

ALSO BY DANIEL KENNEY

THE SCIENCE INSPECTORS SERIES

THE HISTORY MYSTERY KIDS SERIES

PIRATE NINJA AND FRIENDS SERIES

THE BIG LIFE OF REMI MULDOON

TEENAGE TREASURE HUNTER

KATIE PLUMB & THE PENDLETON GANG

I WON'T GIVE UP

YOU CAN FACE YOUR FEARS

I WANT TO FIX THE MOON

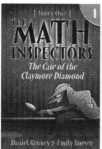

When the Claymore Diamond is stolen from Ravensburg's finest jewelry store, Stanley Carusoe gets the bright idea that he and his friends should start a detective agency.

Armed with curiosity and their love for math, Stanley, Charlotte, Gertie and Felix race around town in an attempt to solve the mystery. Along the way, they butt heads with an ambitious police chief, uncover dark secrets, and drink lots of milkshakes at Mabel's Diner. But when their backs are against the wall, Stanley and his friends rely on the one thing they know best: numbers. Because numbers, they never lie.

Sixth-graders Stanley, Charlotte, Gertie and Felix did more than just start a detective agency. Using their math skills and their gut instincts, they actually solved a crime the police couldn't crack. Now the Math Inspectors are called in to uncover the identity of a serial criminal named Mr. Jekyll, whose bizarre (and hilarious) pranks cross the line into vandalism.

But the deeper the friends delve into the crimes, the more they realize why they were asked to help...and it wasn't because of their detective skills.

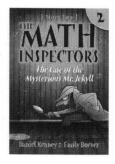

It's Christmas Eve in Ravensburg, and the town is bursting with anticipation for its oldest Christmas tradition. The annual opening of Douglas and Son's Toy Store, home of the greatest toys in the world, is finally here. But this is no ordinary Christmas Eve, and the surprise that awaits them is beyond any of their wildest imaginations: a surprise that threatens to ruin Christmas!

Stanley, Charlotte, Gertie and Felix call in a little backup, but will the team's detective skills and math smarts be enough to unravel the mystery?

Summer vacation has finally arrived, and the Math Inspectors deserve a break. After all, their sixth-grade year was a busy one. On top of all the normal school stuff, Stanley, Charlotte, Gertie, Felix, and Herman made quite a name for themselves as amateur detectives. But when a relaxing day of roller coasters, riddle booths, and waffle eating contests turns into a desperate scramble to save a beloved landmark, the friends quickly discover that this case may be asking more than they are willing to give.

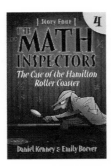

In fact, there may only be one way out—to quit. Will this be the end of the Math Inspectors?

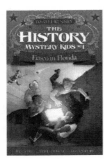

Where did Professor Abner Jefferson go? Before they can find out, April, Henry, and Toad find themselves transported back in time to colonial Florida. Now they have to figure out what's going on, where their father is, and how to get home. Can they find the missing pieces to the puzzle or will they be stuck in history forever?

The History Mystery Kids 1: Fiasco in Florida is the first book in an exciting new time travel series meant for children who have already been reading chapter books and are ready for something more advanced. In each book, this funny, adventuresome series transports children back in time to one of America's 50 states.

The kids at Archie Beller's new school are the weirdest kids in America. Because in Kings Cove, California, kids don't do things like ride bikes, play video games, and read comic books. **Nope, in Kings Cove you're either a Pirate, or you're a Ninja.** And Archie... well, he just wants to be a normal kid from Nebraska. But when these weird kids force Archie to choose a side, **something goes horribly wrong.** Will Archie find his way out of trouble so he can lead the life of a normal kid? Or will he be forced into leading a double life? By day, a normal quiet kid. By night, America's newest crime fighter, a brave superhero known to friend and foe as... PIRATE NINJA!!!

For ten year-old Remi Muldoon, being SMALL is a BIG problem--especially with the kids at school.

And when Remi's attempt to become popular upsets the balance of the universe, things get worse. MUCH worse. Now, Remi must race against the clock to fix history before it's too late and along the way, he might just learn that the smallest of kids can have the biggest of lives.

Brought to life by Author/Illustrator Daniel Kenney, this hilarious first book in the Big Life graphic novel series is perfect for children ages 7-10.

Six months after his mom's death, a still broken-hearted Curial Diggs discovers that she has left him a challenge.

His mom wants him to find The Romanov Dolls, a fantastic treasure stolen from the Manhattan Art Collective when she was only a child. Despite having an overbearing famous father - who has already mapped out his son's future - Curial follows his heart and his mother's clues to Russia where he teams up with the granddaughter of a Russian History Professor to unravel the mystery behind the priceless treasure. Full of history, humor, and danger, Teenage Treasure Hunter is perfect for readers ages 10-14.

ABOUT THE AUTHORS

DANIEL KENNEY

Daniel Kenney is the children's author behind such popular series as *Pirate Ninja & Friends*, *The Big Life of Remi Muldoon*, *The History Mystery Kids*, *The Science Inspectors*, and *The Math Inspectors*. He and his wife live in Omaha, Nebraska, where they enjoy screaming children, little sleep, and dragons. Because who doesn't love dragons? To learn more go to www.DanielKenneyBooks.com.

EMILY BOEVER

Emily Boever was born with an overactive imagination. She spent much of her childhood convinced she was The Incredible Hulk and adventuring with three imaginary friends. When she grew too old to play with friends no one else could see, she turned her imagination to more mature things like studying, traveling, and teaching. Only after marrying her wonderful husband, Matt, and having kids of her own did Emily discover that she was finally old enough to reunite with her imaginary friends (and even add a few new ones) in the pages of her own books. Emily and Matt live with their kids in Omaha, Nebraska. Find more information at www.EmilyBoever.com.

Made in the USA
Middletown, DE
12 October 2020

21776865R00123